Amy Cross is the author of more than 250 horror, paranormal, fantasy and thriller novels.

OTHER TITLES BY AMY CROSS INCLUDE

1689
American Coven
Angel
Anna's Sister
Annie's Room
Asylum
B&B
Bad News
The Curse of the Langfords
Daisy
The Devil, the Witch and the Whore
Devil's Briar
Eli's Town
Escape From Hotel Necro
The Farm
Grave Girl
The Haunting of Blackwych Grange
The Haunting of Nelson Street
The House Where She Died
I Married a Serial Killer
Little Miss Dead
Mary
One Star
Perfect Little Monsters & Other Stories
Stephen
The Soul Auction
Trill
Ward Z
Wax
You Should Have Seen Her

THE CURSE OF BLOODACRE FARM

THE SMYTHE TRILOGY BOOK TWO

AMY CROSS

This edition
first published by Blackwych Books Ltd
United Kingdom, 2024

Copyright © 2024 Blackwych Books Ltd

All rights reserved. This book is a work of fiction.
Names, characters, places, incidents and businesses are
the product of the author's imagination or are
used fictitiously. Any resemblance to actual persons,
living or dead, or to actual events or locations,
is entirely coincidental.

Also available in e-book format.

www.amycross.com
www.blackwychbooks.com

CONTENTS

CHAPTER ONE
page 15

CHAPTER TWO
page 23

CHAPTER THREE
page 31

CHAPTER FOUR
page 41

CHAPTER FIVE
page 49

CHAPTER SIX
page 57

CHAPTER SEVEN
page 65

CHAPTER EIGHT
page 73

CHAPTER NINE
page 81

CHAPTER TEN
page 89

CHAPTER ELEVEN
page 97

CHAPTER TWELVE
page 105

CHAPTER THIRTEEN
page 113

CHAPTER FOURTEEN
page 121

CHAPTER FIFTEEN
page 129

CHAPTER SIXTEEN
page 137

CHAPTER SEVENTEEN
page 145

CHAPTER EIGHTEEN
page 153

CHAPTER NINETEEN
page 161

CHAPTER TWENTY
page 169

CHAPTER TWENTY-ONE
page 177

CHAPTER TWENTY-TWO
page 185

CHAPTER TWENTY-THREE
page 193

CHAPTER TWENTY-FOUR
page 201

CHAPTER TWENTY-FIVE
page 209

CHAPTER TWENTY-SIX
page 219

CHAPTER TWENTY-SEVEN
page 227

CHAPTER TWENTY-EIGHT
page 235

CHAPTER TWENTY-NINE
page 245

CHAPTER THIRTY
page 253

THE CURSE OF BLOODACRE FARM

CHAPTER ONE

January 1ˢᵗ, 1828...

RAIN CRASHED DOWN THROUGH the night air, battering the forest and turning the dirt road into little more than a river of mud. The actual river had almost burst its banks by this point, such had been the intensity of the awful weather that had gripped much of the country since Christmas, and the nearby forest hummed and hissed with the sound of more and more rainfall.

Traipsing through the mud, John Lord made for an unlikely sight as he approached the stone bridge. He'd been a big, strong man once, but now in his late fifties his back had begun to give out and he was more of a hunched and somewhat ruined figure. Had the rain not been so loud, John's ragged breaths would have been a clear sign that something was also wrong with his lungs; he'd walked a couple of miles from his home in the forest, and he was starting to let out a series of gasped, wheezing breaths as he stopped on the bridge and looked down at the pitch-black river raging below.

Over his shoulder, John was carrying a large sack filled with a mass of small writhing bodies.

Letting out a sigh, he hauled the sack down onto the top of the low wall that ran along the side of the bridge. Even above the sound of the rain and the groan of his own labored breaths, he could hear the half dozen kittens mewing and crying out inside the sack. He thought for a moment of how hard he'd had to struggle to get them all in there, and deep down he felt sure that they'd known what was coming. Even at their young age, just a few days old, they clearly had an understanding of death already. They'd been panicking wildly during the final round-up. And that, he told himself, was all the more reason to get this over with.

Reaching down, he fumbled for a moment before finding some large rocks on the ground. He set the rocks on the wall, and then he began to carefully untie the top of the sack while making sure to keep the little bastards from escaping. Sure enough, he felt one of them immediately trying to wriggle through the opening, and he had to slam his fist down to force it back. Grabbing one of the larger rocks, he dropped it into the bag, and then he added the others. Once the bag was heavy enough, he reached down and began to tie it shut again so that -

Suddenly a small black paw lashed out from the top of the sack, its claws catching John's hand. Wincing, he pulled his hand back, but he could already feel rain washing blood from the thick cut. He saw one of the kittens trying desperately to crawl its way out of the sack, and in a moment of unbridled anger he slammed his fist down hard, hitting the creature's head and pushing it back down to join its brothers and sisters. Then, before it or any of the others had a chance to make another bid for freedom, he tied the sack shut again.

"That'll teach me for being kind," he snarled. "I could've just bashed your heads open, but I wanted to make it quicker and less painful for you. And this is the thanks I get, huh?"

He took a deep breath, staring down at the wriggling bag.

"Let this show you," he sneered, "that God isn't real. Not for you, and certainly not for a poor wretched bastard like me."

With that, he gave the bag a hard shove. He leaned over the wall just in time to see the wriggling mass tumbling down and crashing into the dark, raging river below, and sure enough after just a fraction of a second the bag of cats was gone entirely. For a few seconds John imagined the bag sinking into the depths, weighed down by all the rocks. Sure, the cats would be struggling frantically as water filled the bag, but they'd be dead soon enough and their little bodies could simply turn to rotten mush down there on the riverbed.

Turning away and starting the long trudge home, John told himself that he had far more important things to worry about. Already he was starting to think about the next season's harvest, and about all the work he'd have to do on his farm once the weather relented and gave him a chance. He couldn't help but wonder what awful crimes he must have committed in a previous life, to be cursed with such a wretched existence now.

***

Down below the bridge, muddy water continued to crash through the night, pushed on by a surge that had begun many miles further upriver. Never before – certainly not in living memory, at least – had the banks of this particular stretch of the river broken so spectacularly, with water threatening to spill over onto neighboring fields.

Suddenly one of the old oak trees by the side of the river came crashing down, hitting the water with such force that the sound could briefly be heard above the howling storm. The tree had come away at the roots, its surrounding soil having been turned to little more than a muddy bog. The storm was so strong now that it had begun to reshape the landscape, to bring down trees that had stood for over a century. This was far from the first tree that had been toppled on that calamitous night, and other fragments of old branches were already flowing freely along the river's course, remnants of trees further to the south that had also been brought down. Now, however, the huge oak tree was starting to block the river's flow, forcing the water to rise higher on either side and bringing strange new currents and eddies that seemed to go almost against the course of nature.

Finally, over on the far side of the river, something moved in the mud, glistening as it dragged itself out from the raging water. Tiny and weak, barely able to move at all, a solitary black kitten had somehow escaped from the sack when the falling oak had torn the fabric's side, and a second miracle had occurred as this kitten had found itself swept up from the raging depths and had then slammed into the mud. Now it had to use the last of its strength in a desperate attempt to haul itself away from the water. One slip would easily send it tumbling back into the depths, at which point the kitten would surely be lost forever.

Once he'd reached a spot several feet above the river, the kitten stopped and tried to get his breath back. Soaked so badly that his fur felt terribly heavy, the kitten couldn't ignore the burning pain in his limbs. There was pain, too, in one side of his jaw, from where an angry fist had slammed into his head and forced him back down into the depths of the bag. The kitten had tried to fight back, had even drawn blood with one of his claws, but seconds later he'd been sent crashing down into the river. Now, half-drowned and near death, he turned and looked back down at the raging black torrent of water that raced past just a few feet further down.

Spotting something else glistening in the mud, the kitten began to tentatively clamber back toward the water. Reaching down, he pawed at the object, finally managing to drag one of his brothers up onto the mud. Using the side of his face, the kitten nudged his brother several times before realizing that there was no hope; the others were clearly all dead, with most of them no doubt having been washed away in the flood. For the one surviving kitten, the merest thought of his drowned brothers and sisters was almost too much to bear, although he remembered the sensation of clambering over their bodies as he'd fought his way frantically out of the torn bag. Why, he couldn't help but wonder, had the rest of them not been able to do the same?

A moment later the muddy riverbank began to slip. Almost tumbling back into the water, the kitten turned and scrambled further away, desperate to reach safety even as the water took his brother's body and washed it back into the deluge to join the others.

Once he was clear of the river, the kitten began to make his way carefully through the mud, struggling with each breath but somehow managing to force his way through the night. Every step felt like agony, but any rest – even for a moment – would surely lead to death. Instead of allowing himself to weaken, therefore, the kitten forced himself to keep going until he reached the rough path leading up from the river, and finally he managed to get all the way up onto the stone bridge. Here, no longer able to push, the kitten collapsed onto his side and lay gasping for breath in the rain.

No matter how hard he tried to force himself to keep going, he'd reached the absolute limit of his abilities and in that moment he knew that he could go no further.

As rain continued to fall, the kitten lay dying at the side of the road, waiting for the final end that now seemed to have been merely postponed for a few minutes.

CHAPTER TWO

THE FOLLOWING MORNING, WITH the storm having finally abated and the rain having stopped, a cart's wooden wheels splashed through one of the many puddles on the road leading into Almsford.

Struggling as he pulled the cart, Thomas Smith almost slipped, and he quickly muttered a prayer of thanks as he managed to stay upright. His cart was loaded with items he'd bought from a local barn, but Thomas had made this journey many times before and usually had no difficulties; this time, however, the muddy road was proving much more treacherous and he was starting to feel an aching pain in his ankles.

And then, as he stopped for a moment to get his breath back, he spotted a small black shape on the ground nearby, just before the crest of the bridge.

"Hello," he muttered, setting the cart's arms down before making his way over to get a better look. "And what have we got here, then?"

Crouching down, he peered more closely at the soaked pile of fur on the ground. He craned his neck to get a better look at the creature's other side, but he saw no sign of movement.

"Poor thing," he said with a heavy sigh. "Must've drowned in the rain. Can't say that I'm surprised, the air was thick with it last night."

He picked up the cat and tossed it into a nearby grass verge, before getting to his feet and heading back over to his cart. At the last second, however, he turned again as he heard a faint rustling sound; he walked back to the verge and parted the grass, and to his astonishment he saw that the bundle of fur was actually alive. The cat – drenched and clearly terribly weak – was trying to drag itself back onto the road, although it was clearly lacking the necessary strength and after a few seconds it stopped, panting desperately for air.

"Well," Thomas said, raising both eyebrows, "you're certainly a persistent little thing, aren't you?"

Reaching down, he picked the cat up again

and held it in the light. He saw a small face, with eyes that could barely stay open, but there was no denying the fact that the animal was somehow still breathing.

"I think such determination should be rewarded," he continued. "I certainly can't leave you here to die, can I? That means I only have one choice."

Carrying the cat over to the cart, he tossed the animal into one of the boxes, and he watched for a moment as it wriggled and tried in vain to stand.

"You're lucky I came along," he pointed out. "I don't reckon you'd have lasted more than another hour or so. And to be honest, you don't look like you're out of danger just yet. Still, I'll take you home and my wife can see about fattening you up. We've always had a vermin problem on the farm, and I suppose a cat might be useful. I should warn you, though, that you'll have to work for your supper."

Looking up at him, the cat struggled to keep its eyes open before letting out a faint, barely audible mewling sound.

"Save that for when we get home," Thomas said with a grin, turning and picking up the cart's arms again, before setting off on his way. "Let's see if you're any good at mousing."

***

"He's not exactly very big," Mary muttered, holding the cat up in a somewhat ungainly position as she turned him around in the kitchen. "He's just a kitten. Barely even that."

"So not much of a mouser, then?" Thomas suggested, watching from the doorway.

"I think the mouse might be the one to eat *him*," Mary suggested. "I suppose I can try to nurse him to health, and then we'll see where we go from there. Just don't hold out too much hope, because I'm really not getting much of a sense of him."

"Poor thing was by the side of the road," Thomas said, watching as Mary carried the cat over to the far end of the room. "I'm surprised he was still alive. At first, I thought he wasn't."

Mary set the cat down and grabbed a saucer from the side. The cat, meanwhile, managed to stand for a moment before his legs gave way; slumping down, he tried again and again to get up, finally tottering on his four legs as if he simply refused to stay down. A few seconds later, however, the effort proved too much and he once again slithered over.

"Try this," Mary said, setting a saucer of

milk down, then picking the cat up by the scruff of his neck and moving him closer. "The first few days'll be the most important, they'll determine whether or not it lasts."

The cat began to drink from the saucer, but even this effort seemed almost too much. Still unable to stand, he half-sat before dropping down again with some specks of milk on the fur of his face.

"That's not a good start," Mary observed. "There's only so much you can help in these situations, if it can't fend for itself soon then -"

Before she could finish, she heard footsteps hurrying through. She turned just in time to see her daughter Lydia squeezing past Thomas and entering the room.

"Did you get anything from the village?" Lydia asked excitedly, before stopping as soon as she spotted the exhausted cat. "What's that?"

"Your father found it nearly drowned out there near the river," Mary explained, as Thomas made his way back out into the yard. "Don't go getting excited, Lydia, because it's a weak and feeble runt. If I had to guess, I'd say it won't last much longer, but we'll give it a try and see whether it can pull its weight as a mouser." She gave the cat a nudge with the side of her boot, trying to encourage him to drink a little more. "It certainly won't be much good with rats, but eventually it might aspire to killing a mouse or two."

"Can we keep him?" Lydia asked, her voice filled with a sense of wonder as she stepped over and knelt to get a closer look at the cat. "Mother, please, can we? We have so many rats."

"I just told you, didn't I?" she replied, heading to the counter. "It's in the Lord's hands now."

"Is he a little boy?"

"So your father says."

"Does he have a name?"

"You're full of questions today, aren't you?" Mary sighed, clearly tiring of the conversation already as she began to sort through a box of vegetables. "I don't know if it has a name, but if it does, then it certainly didn't bring it with it. Cat seems like a good enough name to me."

"Cat?"

Lydia reached out and gently picked the cat up, holding him in her arms as she looked down into his exhausted eyes.

"I think we can do better than that," she continued. "Why don't we call him Smith?"

"That's a boring name, if you ask me," Mary said, banging some pots about as she made space to start cooking, causing the animal to flinch. "Cat's better."

"Something a little posher than Smith, then," Lydia continued. "What about... oh, I don't know. Why is it so difficult?"

"Call it what you want," Mary muttered. "It's not like it'll know."

"I'll come up with something," Lydia said with a furrowed brow, stroking the cat gently as he rested in her arms. "If you're going to grow up and be big and strong, then I think you need a big and strong name. One with some character. You can trust me to think of one."

Over by the counter, Mary rolled her eyes.

"You'll get used to it here," Lydia continued. "You're just a kitty now, but soon you'll grow up to be big and strong, and then you'll be the scourge of any mouse or rat that dares set foot on the farm. I've got total faith in you."

"Have you finished cleaning those barrels?" Mary asked, her voice filled with a sense of suspicion. "I don't want you sitting around playing with that cat if there's still work you haven't completed."

"I'm nearly done," Lydia said, lifting the saucer up and holding it so that the cat could drink. "There you go," she continued, watching as the creature finally managed to get some liquid. "Mother, I just need to help him a little first. There's no -"

"I need those barrels cleaned *now*!" Mary snapped, pulling the cat from her daughter's hands, throwing him across the room and setting the saucer on the counter, before grabbing the girl's wrist and dragging her toward the door. "You can be a lazy little thing sometimes, Lydia Smith, but you're going to finish your tasks. Do you see me sitting around doing nothing? What about your father? Of course you don't. That's because we have to work to make this farm run properly, and you're a big part of that. Your father purchased some boxes from the old Smythe farm and he needs to sort through it all. You never know, he might've actually found something valuable this time!"

Mary's voice continued to ring out from the yard as the cat tried again to get to his feet. He was struggling just as much as before, at least for a few seconds until he finally managed to stand properly. He tried to haul himself across the cobbled floor, before finally slumping back down again. Outside, Mary was shouting louder than ever at her daughter.

CHAPTER THREE

TWO WEEKS LATER, THE cat stood in the grass at the end of the family's yard and watched as a mouse scurried past the wall. Staying completely still for a few seconds, the animal kept his gaze fixed firmly on the mouse for a few more seconds before suddenly leaping into action, missing the mouse by a few inches and instead slamming into the wall.

The mouse, meanwhile, quickly disappeared into a hole in the very same wall.

"That's okay," Lydia said, stepping over and reaching down to stroke the cat's side. "You're still so new to this. You'll work it out eventually."

Purring gently, the cat pushed against her hand.

"I bet there are a million mice on this farm," Lydia continued. "Mother says they're always chewing holes in things. There are probably rats and stoats, too. Once you're fully grown, you'll be busy with them all day." She paused, before raising her right hand slightly. "Do you remember this trick I was showing you yesterday?"

The cat stared back at her.

"Wave," she continued, moving her hand very gently from side to side. "Remember? You almost had it. Wave at me."

The cat hesitated, before slowly lifting his right paw as if he was about to copy her movement. At the last second, however, he stopped as if he'd forgotten the next part.

"Wave," Lydia said with a growing smile. "You can -"

"Lydia!" Mary barked as she emerged from the back of the house. "What are you doing over there?"

"I have to do my chores," Lydia sighed. "I wish I could just play with you all day instead. Father's off looking for more scrap in one of the villages, and when he gets back he'll want me to help sort through it all. I hate the fact that we make our living by going through things that other people have thrown away. Sometimes I think we're *never* going to be rich."

Still purring, the cat turned and pressed his other side against Lydia's hand.

"Now!" Mary snapped, having stormed over. She grabbed Lydia by the scruff of the neck and hauled her up, before spinning her round and shoving her hard, causing her to trip and almost fall down. "Ever since that filthy animal showed up, young girl, you've been slacking! I'm starting to wish your father had never brought it here in the first place!"

As Lydia hurried over to the stable, Mary turned and saw that the cat was starting to track another mouse. Watching carefully, Mary waited as the mouse edged slightly closer; the cat was completely still once more, preparing to pounce, and Mary tilted her head slightly as she began to wonder whether finally the wretched little monster might show some initiative. A moment later the cat lurched forward, grabbing the mouse and flinging it into the air; as soon as the mouse landed, the cat tried to grab it again, only to let out a cry of pain as the mouse bit his leg hard. Pulling back, the cat began to limp away as the mouse darted back into the barn.

"The mouse bit you," Mary sighed. "That's the wrong way round, you stupid little scrap of fur."

Grabbing the cat, she hauled him up and saw blood glistening on one of his legs. "That's it, I'm out of patience. You've done nothing but cause trouble since you came here. You're no mouser, and Lydia's ignoring her duties." She hesitated as the cat struggled to get free, and then she turned and carried him around to the side of the house.

Reaching one of the water butts, she pulled the lid off and looked down at the surface of the dark, stagnant liquid.

"I've never been one for animals," she continued, as the cat tried again and again to slip out of her grasp. "I'm not feeding another mouth, no matter how small it might be, if it doesn't contribute anything." She held the cat up and looked into his eyes. "You've had your chance, but you're far too weak. Consider this a blessing. You wouldn't have lived a happy life anyway. Let this teach you that God is real, and that there's mercy in this world."

With that, she plunged the cat beneath the surface, holding him under as he struggled frantically. Refusing to budge, Mary pushed him even deeper and tightened her grip on his throat, and eventually she felt him starting to weaken once more. She looked into the water, but she couldn't see much down past her own elbow; she could feel the cat losing its battle, however, although the creature lasted longer than she'd expected before finally its struggles faded to nothing. She held him under for a good minute longer, just to be certain, before finally lifting him up and peering at his face. Sure enough, she saw his dead eyes staring back at her.

"Good riddance," she muttered as water dribbled down from the corpse's fur. "You were no -"

"What are you doing?" Lydia gasped, rushing over and trying to grab the cat from her mother's hands. "Don't hurt him!"

"Stop that!" Mary snapped, slapping her daughter hard and pushing her away. "How dare you talk to your own mother with such a wicked tongue? Don't you know your place?"

"What did you do?" Lydia sobbed as she saw the dead cat. "Why did you kill him?"

"Everything has to earn its place in this world," Mary said firmly. "This thing was never going to be a mouser, so do you know the only way it can help us?" She turned and threw the dead animal into the nearby bushes. "As fertilizer," she added with a chuckle, before setting the lid back onto the water butt. "I was already far too lenient with you, but it's about time you learned a valuable lesson. Now, how about we get back to normal and you do your chores properly? I've had enough silliness for one week."

"But he was my friend," Lydia whimpered, with tears streaming down her face as she stared at the bushes. "You don't understand, he was going to -"

Before she could finish, Mary slapped her again, much harder this time.

"Don't you dare answer back to me!" she hissed, grabbing the girl by the ear and dragging her back around to the other side of the house. "Your father might be soft with you, but I'm going to make sure you're raised right! And that means putting you to work!"

***

"Well," Thomas said that evening, after a long silence at the dinner table, "I'm sure it's for the best, anyway. Lydia, you must remember that your mother's word is final in these matters."

Sniffing back more tears, Lydia stared down at the untouched boiled vegetables on her plate.

"It's my fault," Thomas added, "for bringing it here in the first place. I shouldn't have done that, I should have recognized that it -"

"He wasn't an *it*!" Lydia snapped angrily.

"He was my cat!"

"Don't talk to your father that way," Mary said firmly.

"But it's true!" Lydia protested. "He wasn't just a thing, he was a cat and he was really young and he was alive! You didn't give him long enough to prove himself, but he would've been able to catch mice eventually. Father, he was still learning!"

"Are you going to let her talk to you like that?" Mary asked, turning to Thomas.

"The girl's just upset," he replied calmly.

"That doesn't give her the right to talk to her own parents in such a way," Mary continued. "If I'd done that to my own father, he'd have used a cane on me! If this girl doesn't learn her lesson soon, she'll be completely out of control."

"My dear," Thomas said with a heavy sigh, "I think she just -"

"Are you a good father or not?" Mary added, cutting him off. "It's bad enough that I had to be the one to bring this sorry chapter to a close by drowning the little beast. Are you now going to sit there and let our own daughter disrespect us in such a manner? How's she ever going to find herself a husband if she thinks she could talk to her betters like this?"

"Who says I even *want* a husband?" Lydia

replied.

"Did you hear that?" Mary gasped, still waiting for Thomas to react. "What kind of father are you, if you can't even discipline your own daughter?"

"Fine," Thomas muttered, getting to his feet. "Lydia, meet me in the front room. You know what I'm going to have to do."

"But Father -"

"Enough!" he shouted, before taking a moment to compose himself. "Mary, fetch the birch from the kitchen, and Lydia you must know that you'll be taking ten lashes for such poor behavior. And if you answer back in any way, I'll double that number. Have I made myself clear?"

"I just don't think that it's fair!" Lydia sobbed.

"Twenty lashes," he told her.

"Thirty," Mary said as she got to her feet and made her way to the kitchen. "That's the only way to teach children. My own father caned me on the backside once, and let me assure you that I never behaved badly again. While you're administering this punishment, Thomas, I shall pray to the Lord that our daughter might yet learn how to control herself."

"Are you really going to cane me, Father?"

Lydia asked once Mary had left the room. "I didn't do anything wrong!"

"Your heard your mother," Thomas said darkly. "Go and prepare yourself. Bend over the chair in the corner. I shall be through shortly to administer your thirty lashes."

***

Darkness had fallen several hours earlier. A moment later the silence was broken by the sound of a cane hitting human flesh, accompanied by Lydia's pained cry; a few seconds after that, the same pair of sounds rang out again.

In the dark bushes, the cat's drowned corpse lay far away from any moonlight. Already, insects had begun to eat their way through his flesh, burrowing into his body with the intent of hollowing him from the inside out.

CHAPTER FOUR

10 years later...

"THIS MIGHT BE WORTH something," Thomas said as he began to lift an old dresser from the back of his cart. "I think I might even be able to -"

Before he could get another word out, the weight shifted and he gasped as the dresser began to fall. At the very last second, however, a figure rushed over and threw itself against the dresser, holding it up so that it wouldn't smash down onto the ground.

"I told you to wait for me, Father," Lydia said, adjusting her grip before helping him lower it down properly. "Are you *trying* to cause even more damage to your back?"

"I'm not as young as I once was, that's true,"

Thomas muttered, grateful for the assistance as he placed the dresser on the dirty ground. "I thought I could manage it, that's all. I used to be able to manage this sort of thing easily enough."

He reached over and put a hand on Lydia's arm. She tried to pull away, but his grip was too strong.

"You're a good girl," he added.

She tried to smile, but she hated anyone touching her and she tried again to slip free.

"I hope you know that," he continued, watching her eyes carefully. "You've always been good to me."

He watched her for a moment longer, before finally letting go.

"This looks nice," Lydia replied, quickly stepping around to the other side so that she could inspect the dresser more closely. "Do you remember that one we sold to the gentleman in Cobblefield a few years ago? That's what this reminds me of, except it might be in even better condition. Don't you agree?"

"You might be right," he said, wincing as he touched the small of his back and wiped sweat from his brow. "As you've grown up, my girl, you've developed a real eye for these things."

"You're in pain."

"No, I -"

"If you put your back out entirely," she

continued, "then what will we do? Father, please, go and rest for a while. I can unload everything else." She waited for him to acquiesce. "That's an order."

"Fine," he said, clearly still in pain as he turned and began to limp toward the house. "How's your mother today? Has she been up?"

"She's in bed, as usual," Lydia said as she climbed up onto the back of the cart and began to look at the various boxes her father had acquired on his latest trip. "That's three days in a row she hasn't risen. I know the doctor told us not to worry, but I can't help myself. I fear she's developing sores, but she refuses to let me even turn her."

"Your mother has always been stubborn," he pointed out as he walked away.

"I really don't know what's wrong with her," Lydia said, pulling some of the boxes aside, then looking into one and seeing what appeared to be a bunch of old leather-bound books. Picking one up, she began to flick through the pages, only to see lots of text that she could barely decipher. "This is different to your usual haul, Father," she continued. "If I didn't know better, I'd think you must have got this from someone rather learned. Who exactly do you think might buy it all?"

"I don't know right now," he called back to her as he got closer to the house. "That's your job, Lydia. I'm sure you'll think of something we can do with the stuff."

"I'm sure I shall," she muttered, still flicking through the book, absorbed by the beautiful illustrations that seemed to show various plants and liquid mixtures. "Of course, the trouble will be finding someone in these parts who can actually read."

***

Half a dozen mice raced across the bedroom floor, squeaking loudly until two of them collided and began to fight. The squeaks continued until one of the mice let out a cry of pain, before a wooden stick slammed down from above and almost squashed them. At this, the mice all hurried away, some going into a hole in the wall while others took refuge under the bed.

"Horrible vermin!" Mary cried out, slamming her stick down several more times in a vain attempt to kill at least one of the mice. "Won't they ever leave me in peace?"

"Mother?"

After knocking gently, Lydia pushed the door open and saw that her mother was still lashing out with the stick, attempting to hit the mice even though they'd all already scattered.

"Mother, that won't help," Lydia continued, setting a plate of food down on the table next to the bed, then hurrying over and trying to pull the stick from the old woman's hands. "Mother, I think -"

"Leave me alone!" Mary snapped, lashing out at her daughter instead, hitting her several times on the leg in an attempt to force her back. "I don't want you in here! Do you hear me? I just want to get rid of these mice, they're everywhere! They used to be just downstairs but now they even get up here, they terrorize me all times of the day and night, and do you and your father care? Not one jot!"

"I'll put down some more poison," Lydia muttered, heading back around the bed and picking up the plate, then holding it out for her. "Here, take -"

"I'm not hungry!" Mary shouted, pushing the plate away and sending it crashing down onto the floor, spilling the gruel across the wooden boards. A couple of mice immediately ran out to steal some crumbs. "How many times do I have to tell you? If I'm hungry, I'll tell you!"

"At least let me see to your sores," Lydia replied, stepping closer and pulling the bed-sheets aside, revealing thick weltering patches of reddened skin on her mother's bare side, with pus having soaked out into the sheets. "You can't stay like this," she continued, lifting up some of the flaps of skin, only to find that they were partially stuck to the fabric. "Mother, you're going to become very sick if -"

"Leave me alone!" Mary screamed, lashing

out with the stick, hitting Lydia on the chest and pushing her back again. Reaching down, she moved the sheets over to cover her nakedness. "Did I ask you to interfere? I'm your mother, young lady, and you'd do well to remember that I know best!"

"You haven't left that bed for days," Lydia reminded her. "Your pot -"

"You can empty my pot when it needs emptying," Mary snarled, leaning back on her pillows. "You'll know soon enough when that moment arrives." She placed a hand on the front of the sheets, above her swollen belly. "Not that much has come out of late. I try and I try, but it's like it's all blocked somehow."

"That's why you need -"

"I need to rest!" Mary hissed. "It's alright for you, you're young, you don't know what it's like to spend a lifetime working, only to have your body fail you!" She wiped some tears from the sides of her eyes. "You think it's all so easy, but your time'll come! You and your father, you'll both see the truth eventually!"

"I just want to help," Lydia said through clenched teeth, reminding herself that she shouldn't judge anyone, let alone her own mother. "If you'd just -"

"Lord knows, I've suffered," Mary continued, looking up at the ceiling. "Lord knows, I've tried to do the right thing, and what's my reward? An ungrateful husband and a terrible daughter who's been nothing but a disappointment. Sometimes I think you want me to just rot away in this bed!"

"I want nothing of the sort," Lydia replied as she scooped the food back onto the plate and headed to the door. "I'm going to tend to Father, he's hurt his back again but -"

"Liar!" Mary snapped angrily. "He's always pretending to be injured. Well, you can tell him that this time I won't be stepping in to make everything better! Tell him he's got to pull himself together for once!"

"I'll be back up later," Lydia told her, "and then I really think we ought to try to get you out of that bed, if only for a few minutes so that I can clean you and change the sheets." She paused for a moment, keenly aware of a sickly sweet smell in the air, worried that her mother's sores might be even worse than she'd realized. "I know that's not what you want," she added, "but I really can't leave you like this for much longer. If I promise to make sure not to hurt you, Mother, will you let me at least try to help?"

"Ungrateful, sniveling little cow," Mary murmured under her breath. "Always thinking yourself superior, aren't you? I see it in your eyes all the time. You think you're so much better than me, but you're not! You're just a spiteful little monster,

I'll be lucky if you don't turn out to be a common whore when you're older!"

Lydia opened her mouth to reply, but instead she hesitated for a moment. She desperately wanted to defend herself, but deep down she knew that there was no point.

"I'll be back up later," she said finally, before taking the plate and leaving the room, bumping the door shut as she went.

"Lord," Mary said, staring up at the ceiling, "won't you deliver me from these devils? I've been your faithful servant my whole life. Please, I'm begging you... cast my husband and daughter down, give them *my* afflictions so that I can be better again. Then we'll see who's laughing!"

As she continued to offer her depraved prayer, she paid no attention to the mice that had emerged from under the bed to collect scraps of the food that she'd spilled. She didn't even notice as those mice dragged the food back into the darkness beneath her, where many more tiny mouths could be heard chewing.

CHAPTER FIVE

"I'VE GOT TO GO to Almsford tomorrow morning," Thomas said, limping more heavily than before as he made his way into the front room after dinner. Still touching the small of his back, he stopped for a moment and let out a gasp of pain. "I'll be gone for most of the day."

"You'll do no such thing," Lydia replied, examining another of the books by candlelight. "If you need anything from Almsford, I shall go in your place."

"You can't possibly pull a cart full of things all the way back to the farm."

"Then I'll find someone who can."

"Lydia -"

"Do you have anything specific to pick up?" she asked, turning to him. "Or are you just going to hunt around for more items you think you can sell?"

"I don't see why that matters," he said a little defensively. "I just thought I'd see if there's anything available, that's all. You never know what people might have discarded at the side of the road."

"*I* shall go to Almsford tomorrow and run some errands," she told him. "While I'm there, I shall keep an eye out. If there's anything worth having, I'll ask them to keep it until you're well enough to fetch it. That seems like a perfectly reasonable way of doing things."

"Should only be a day or two," he said gruffly, before watching for a moment as his daughter continued to examine one of the books. "What have you got there?"

"You should know," she replied. "You brought them back here."

"Yes, but I didn't really bother to look at them," he muttered, limping over to the table and picking up one of the other books. "They seem pretty old, I'm really not sure that anyone'll give us much for them. And they seem stuffed full of nonsense."

"They're beautiful," she pointed out, turning to another page and seeing another set of illustrations. "Some of these are hand-drawn. The language is a little difficult to decipher, a lot of it's in Latin or something else that I can't possibly understand. Father, don't you remember where you found them?"

"There were a few houses with things left out the side," he explained. "I only took what was being freely given away. I suppose these books came from one of those piles, but you can't expect me to remember any details. I'm not much into books, anyway, and -"

Before he could finish, he winced again. This time Lydia got to her feet and helped him into a nearby chair, taking care to avoid hurting him even more as she put an arm around his waist and gently lowered him down until he was a little more comfortable.

"I'm fine," he spluttered. "You don't need to make a fuss."

"You're sick and -"

"I told you, I'm fine!" he hissed, pushing her away with more force than usual, then letting out a heavy sigh. "I'm sorry, I didn't mean to do that," he added. "It's just that I'm not used to being fussed over. Your mother always tells me to push through the pain, and I've got a feeling she's right on the money there. No man ever prospered by sitting on his backside." He began to try to stand again, only for the pain to strike and force him back down. "I don't take well to injury," he muttered. "I've never let myself get stopped before."

"I shall make you something to drink,"

Lydia replied, heading toward the doorway before stopping and hurrying back to grab the book. "Wait right here. If you push too hard, you'll only hurt yourself more. If you really want to get back up on your feet, the best thing right now is some good honest rest."

***

Another candle flickered on the bench, casting its dancing light across the pages of the tattered old book as Lydia stirred some more sugar into the mixture she was preparing.

"One of Mother's favorite old recipes," she said under her breath, before glancing at the book and seeing its beautiful but illegible text. "I wish I could read you," she added, with a hint of sadness in her voice. "Your illustrations are so beautiful, but whatever language you're written in, I haven't got the learning to know what it says. I wish I could read Latin or... whatever that is."

She stared down at the book for a moment longer, before heading to the shelves on the far side of the room and pulling one of them open. Reaching up to take a jar of honey, she winced as she felt a flickering pain on one side of her head. She paused as the sensation faded away, and she quickly told herself that there was nothing to worry about.

Opening the door of a nearby cupboard, she

reached inside for a jar, only to let out a gasp and pull back. Spotting blood on her finger, she looked into the cupboard just in time to see a rat scurrying through a hole that led into the wall.

"Filthy things," she sighed, before taking the jar out and then closing the door.

She took a moment to clean the cut on her finger.

"Such a long day," she muttered, carrying the honey back to the counter. "I fear -"

A shock of pain returned, this time darting across her skull from one temple to the other. She stopped and gritted her teeth; the pain was already gone, yet it had left an echo that seemed to be rippling through her mind. As she looked down at the counter, she was shocked to see that the surface was swimming slightly, as if warped by some outside force; at the same time, a flickering halo of light had appeared in her vision, obscuring part of the counter.

"Another headache," she whispered, having experienced similar things before. "The timing couldn't be worse. I certainly don't have a spare moment in which to be sick."

She waited, but now the light was getting larger, filling her eyes. These strange headaches had struck her in the past, usually coming about twice a year and seemingly brought on by moments of great stress; she knew that there was no remedy, that all she could do was wait them out as the familiar cycle of symptoms arrived one by one. First came the flashes of pain, then the lights in her eyes, and then she often felt a sense of nausea combined with some numbness on the left side of her body. Sometimes this numbness extended not only along her arm but also up to her face, including her tongue. Her mother had told her to stop fussing, and had insisted that she too experienced the same headaches from time to time, that women in their family had been plagued by such things for as long as anyone could remember. Soon, Lydia knew, the numbness would give way to a sense of light confusion, as if her mind had been filled with fog, and then the symptoms would fade to leave only a pounding headache that could last for up to a day. Occasionally a kind of sensitivity to light came too, and she knew she should try to get some sleep in a darkened room, but usually she had to simply push on through and try to hide the fact that she was poorly at all.

"Just a few more minutes," she said out loud, as the flashing lights filled her eyes and kept her from seeing much of anything. "Lord, I beg of you that this should be not as bad as before, so that I might better serve Mother and Father. In this trying time, they need me."

She took a deep breath, and sure enough a few minutes later the visual disturbance began to clear. She could already feel a dull throb in the back of her head, but at least the numbness seemed not to be arriving on this occasion. Although she knew she wasn't in the clear yet, she finally resolved to ignore the headache to the best of her ability; instead she focused on spooning some honey from the jar, hoping to get the mixture complete before the inevitable confusion arrived. As she turned the spoon over and over, she glanced at the strange book, and then she froze as she realized that something had changed.

The text, which just minutes earlier had seemed inscrutable and impossible to read, was now as clear as day.

Leaning closer, she squinted slightly, yet still the text remained resolved. She knew that the words had previously appeared to be written in Latin or some other obscure language, yet now everything was presented in the most ordinary English. Even Lydia, with her dearth of formal education, found that she could now read the sentences with no trouble whatsoever.

"I call upon the spirits," she whispered as she read from the page, "to grant me relief from this state, such that I might improve and -"

She turned to the next page, and here too the words were easy to read.

"- and absorb the power of Attaroth," she added, "so that I am able to bring forth my darkest and most devious wishes."

Furrowing her brow, she tried to comprehend what those words could actually mean. They were presented next to a beautiful drawing that seemed to show a flower in the process of opening up. For a moment, with the dull pain still echoing in the back of her skull, Lydia found herself utterly absorbed by the book and its strange words, almost as if the pages were drawing her out of her own world and into something of its own creation.

"Lydia?" her father called out suddenly. "Are you still in there?"

"Yes!" she gasped, looking at the door, then turning to see that she'd allowed honey to leak out from the jar and spread across the counter. "No!"

She grabbed a cloth and tried to clear the mess up, but she succeeded only in spreading the thick, sticky substance all across the counter while some even began to dribble down onto the floor.

"Damn my distraction," she added, fully aware that this would take a while to clear up.

"I'm feeling better now," Thomas continued. "I think I might -"

"No, stay there!" Lydia called out, already trying to work out how she was going to deal with the mess. "Don't move, Father! I've got everything under control!"

CHAPTER SIX

"I'VE GOT EVERYTHING UNDER control," she muttered a couple of hours later, on her knees in the kitchen as she continued to clean up the honey that had spilled just about everywhere. Moonlight was casting strange shadows on the windows above her. "A likely claim."

Still scrubbing the floor, she knew that her father would immediately notice the spilled honey if he made his way down from the spare bedroom. She'd just about managed to shepherd him up there to keep him out of the kitchen, but come morning the sticky mess would surely be impossible to miss. The more she scrubbed, however, the more she began to worry that the honey was stubbornly clinging to the wooden floor, and that it might never be removed entirely. As she adjusted her position slightly, her knees pushed against the boards and she felt a ripple of discomfort; at least the pain in her head wasn't too bad, and she was relieved that the ache seemed to have petered out rather than striking with its usual ferocity.

Above, the ceiling creaked slightly. Lydia froze, worried that her mother might be trying to get out of bed; the sound failed to return, however, and she realized that the old woman was simply shifting her position.

Getting to her feet, she carried the bowl of water across the room and set it down on the counter. She knew she had to keep working, but her knees were burning and she felt herself already weakening; sitting on the chair by the window, she told herself that she would only rest for a minute or two, and that then she'd get back to work. If necessary, she could scrub all night and keep going until the sun came up, and then she'd just have to hide her tiredness from her parents. At that moment she remembered that she'd promised to go to the village, and the idea filled her with a sense of great exhaustion, but deep down she knew that a promise had to be kept. Somehow, she supposed, she would find a way to get through the next day.

Just as she found a way to get through *every* day.

Spotting the old book still resting on the counter, she slid it closer and looked through the pages again. The text was still legible, which surprised her a little, although she had no idea what to make of it all. Finally she stopped at a page that appeared to show an illustration of a figure dragging itself up from a grave; a shudder passed through her chest at such a horrible sight, but she still found herself looking at the words.

"Should you wish to never sleep," she whispered, "I'll pray for you and never weep."

A shiver ran through her bones.

"Though you are dead, you shall yet rise," she continued, "and open up your dusty eyes."

She paused, puzzled by the strange incantation.

"You shall yet walk, as once before," she read, "and cast the dark into the morn."

She swallowed hard.

"And live again," she added finally, "in shadow reborn. Draw life, from others torn."

Now that she'd reached the end of the page, she couldn't help but wonder why she'd even bothered to read such foolish words in the first place. Nevertheless, she read them again, silently this time but trying to understand a little better what they could possibly mean. Although she wanted to dismiss the contents of the book, some deep part of her felt almost as if she'd just stumbled upon something dangerous. She looked again at the illustration, and at the dark figure that was shown clawing its way out from the dirt, and she began to wonder just what kind of book her father had brought into the house.

Closing the tome, she looked at the leather cover. She ran her fingertips against the material, and for a moment she couldn't help but note that this particular book seemed different to all others. At first she couldn't quite work out what was causing this sensation, until she was struck by a sudden and rather awful thought. She held the book up, turning it around in the candlelight, until finally she saw that there were indeed what appeared to be a few straggly gray hairs growing out from the book's surface. Horrified, she told herself that she had to be wrong, yet the awful sight persisted until slowly – with a rising sense of dread – Lydia set the book down and pulled her hand away.

Suddenly something thudded against the window, startling her to such an extent that she jumped up and stepped back. The sound had been loud but brief, and after a moment she headed to the back door and pulled it open. She leaned out and looked into the darkness, and she was just about able to make out what appeared to be a small dead blackbird on the ground. The poor thing had evidently flown straight into the windowpane and had broken its neck, although Lydia was surprised that it had been active in the middle of the night.

She looked around the garden, but in the

darkness she saw almost nothing. The air felt colder than usual, however, becoming almost uncomfortable to breathe, and Lydia couldn't shake the sense that somehow the world seemed slightly different. She continued to watch the shadows, but she was increasingly disturbed by an unsettled feeling in her chest, and finally she stepped back and made sure to shut the door firmly.

Making a mental note to bury the bird in the morning, she closed the book on the counter before walking back across the kitchen. She got down onto her painful knees and returned to work, desperately trying to clean up at least a little more of the spilled honey before morning.

***

"Why does nobody come to me? Why am I neglected by everyone?"

Flat on her back in the filthy bed upstairs, Mary could barely raise her voice above a whisper. She'd been shifting her weight every few minutes in the darkness, desperate to get comfortable, yet every move just made her feel worse. She was so terribly tired, yet sleep would not come and she had begun to believe that her best bet might be to rise from the bed and walk around a little, if only to make herself tired. The effort required, however, was proving too much to muster, although as yet she hadn't quite given up.

"Thomas!" she called out, hoping that her husband would come to her. "Get your wretched body out of bed and help me!"

She waited, but she'd heard him going into the spare room earlier and knew that he'd never lift a finger to help his poor long-suffering wife. After all, why would he suddenly start to be a good husband after so many years of failure?

"Lydia!" she shouted, reaching up and banging her fist against the wall. "Girl, I know *you're* awake! I can't sleep! You can't just leave me here in my own filth! I need... I think I need a bath! You have to heat some water and wash me, else I'm liable to fall sick from the stench of my own humors. Do you hear me, Lydia?"

She waited, but already she knew that she was going to be ignored. Telling herself that this was typical, and that she'd always been mistreated by her cruel and ungrateful family, Mary took a moment to gather her remaining strength before once again trying to lift herself up from the bed. This time she made an extra effort to push through the pain, and the candle burning on a nearby windowsill picked out an expression of pure anger on her face; she flinched and girded her loins, and she refused to cease her efforts even as she felt the bed trying to hold her down. After a moment she heard a faint ripping sound, as if something had started tearing through cotton, but she forced herself to keep going and finally she slowly began to rise from the bed.

Beneath her, the flesh of her back had fused with the dirty sheets, and her skin had begun to grow over some of the folds of the fabric. The more she tried to lift herself up, the more Mary began to pull at those joins, ripping her skin and letting more blood and pus dribble down from her back. In places, the flesh had worn so thin that parts of her spine were showing, while small maggots wriggled excitedly through her meat. A few of the maggots dropped down onto the filthy bed-sheets, and more juices quickly rained down upon them as Mary tried over and over again to at least sit up on the bed.

"Lydia!" she screamed finally. "Girl, where are you? I need you to help me!"

***

Out in the pitch-black garden, a hedgehog sniffed its way across the grass, heading toward the bushes at the end of the lawn. As its nose twitched, the hedgehog showed no sign of fear, until suddenly it stopped as it discovered the corpse of a dead rat. It sniffed the rat for a moment before stepping past, only to quickly find the corpse of a small brown bird. Continuing, the hedgehog reached the edge of the lawn and stopped as it heard a slow scratching sound coming from somewhere nearby.

And then, with no warning at all, the hedgehog let out a brief cry of pain before slumping down dead against the grass.

As the scratching sound continued, another hedgehog crossed the lawn, stopping to sniff the various small dead animals. Reaching the first hedgehog, the creature sniffed the corpse for a moment before starting to scurry past, only to suddenly let out a cry of its own and also roll over dead.

Somewhere nearby, a little way beyond the bushes, the scratching sound was getting louder and louder.

CHAPTER SEVEN

"THIS FLOOR SEEMS STICKY," Thomas muttered the following morning, stepping once again onto a floorboard in the kitchen, then lifting his foot and feeling the slightest hint of resistance. "Has something been spilled on it?"

"I don't believe so, Father," Lydia replied, forcing a smile as she chopped vegetables on the counter. Exhausted from a night spent scrubbing, she could barely keep her eyes open. "I'm sure it's nothing."

"Has your mother been downstairs this morning?"

"I'm sure she hasn't," Lydia told him. "How long has it been since she was even able to get out of bed? I'm going to go and wake her soon with something to drink."

"I'm sure she'll be grateful," Thomas said, rolling his eyes as he tested the sticky patch on the floor a few more times. "My back's feeling a lot better already, Lydia. I don't think you'll need to go into the village after all, I should be more than capable of -"

"Let me stop you there," she said firmly, turning to him with the knife still held in her right hand. "Father, I'm glad that you're feeling better, but you really must learn to rest a little. If you go rushing around, you'll only end up feeling worse." She waited for him to reply, but she could already see from the expression on his face that he wasn't fully convinced. "You know I'm right," she added, prodding the air with the knife's tip in an attempt to underline her point. "Please, Father, won't you just listen to me for once?"

"And what am I supposed to do here?" he asked with a sigh. "I'm no cripple, Lydia, and I'm not lazy."

"Nobody in their right mind ever called you lazy *or* a cripple," she told him, "but you're certainly stubborn. Listen, I'm going to finish cutting up these vegetables and then I'm going to go to the village. Meanwhile, you'll stay here and find some way to occupy your time, and then in a day or two you'll be all better. Then you'll be able to get on with your work, and you'll feel so much stronger. Doesn't that sound like a good idea?"

"I suppose so," he murmured.

"I dread to think what you'd be like if you didn't have me here to look after you," she replied, as she got back to work cutting up the rest of the vegetables. "I suppose Mother used to keep an eye on you, but these days she's unable to do much at all." She glanced briefly up at the ceiling before looking at the vegetables again. "I haven't heard any sign of movement coming from the bedroom, but I'm sure she'll be shouting for something soon. Don't worry, though. I'll tend to her before I leave, so you won't have to do anything at all."

"Your mother and I are very lucky to have you, Lydia," Thomas said after a moment's pause. "I hope you know that we appreciate you very much. The day you marry some local boy is the day we really have to worry about looking after ourselves."

"I shouldn't think that I'll ever marry," she replied, trying to hide the hint of sadness that was creeping into her voice. "I don't have time to go courting, and it's not as if an eligible young man is going to drop from the sky and land in my lap."

"I don't want you to be alone when you're older," he told her. "That wouldn't be fair."

"I'm quite content," she told him, and now she was able somehow to make her smile seem that much more convincing. So convincing, in fact, that she almost believed it herself. "Besides, who would ever be able to put up with me?"

***

Stepping out into the back garden, Lydia was already making a mental list of everything she had to do when she reached the village. After a moment, however, she stopped as she spotted several strange dark items over on the far side of the lawn.

"Don't forget to stand your ground!" Thomas called out to her from inside the house. "There'll be people in Almsford who think they can fool you, just because you're a girl!"

"I'll keep that in mind, Father," she replied as she made her way across the lawn. "Don't worry, I won't let..."

Her voice trailed off as she saw that the dark items were actually various small dead animals. Puzzled, she crouched down and saw the corpses of three hedgehogs, half a dozen birds and several rats. None of the bodies showed any obvious sign of injury, but after a moment Lydia took a stick from the ground and used it to turn one of the hedgehogs over; the little creature's eyes were still open, as was its mouth, yet Lydia still saw no blood. As far as she could tell, the various animals appeared to have simply dropped dead in this particular spot near the border; she looked over at the soil and saw that one of the bushes had been disturbed, so she got to her feet and took a closer look.

To her surprise, she found that the soil behind the bush had been pushed aside, as if something had been dug up with a spade. As she leaned down to look closer, in fact, she began to wonder whether the opposite might be true; the patch of freshly-disturbed dirt looked almost as if it had been pushed up from beneath, as if something had forced its way out of the ground. She knew that must be impossible, of course, yet she couldn't help noticing that the bush had been pushed aside as if some kind of object had forced its way through.

"How peculiar," she whispered under her breath, wondering what kind of animal might have done such a thing.

Glancing around, she saw no sign of anything untoward – save for the dead creatures near her feet, at least. She noticed after a moment that she was feeling a curious sense of peace and calm, almost as if the atmosphere in this particular part of the garden had been touched by something from another world. Still she looked around, convinced that something was wrong, and after a few seconds she realized that in fact she felt as if she was being watched. She checked that no-one was at any of the windows, but in truth she already knew that this sensation was rooted in the garden itself, as if something was hidden nearby.

"Hello?" she said cautiously, even though she felt foolish for giving voice to her fears. "Is anyone there?"

She waited. Hearing nothing, she noticed that the garden actually seemed very still, almost as if nothing was moving anywhere at all. She looked first one way and then the other, but still she saw no sign of life. Even the tiny creatures that usually wriggled out of sight seemed to be gone.

"Can anyone hear me?" she continued. "If -"

Stopping herself just in time, she realized that she was allowing her imagination to run wild.

Sighing, she used her right foot to gently roll the dead creatures off the grass and onto the soil. She felt bad for treating the animals in such a manner, but the last thing she wanted was for either of her parents to worry that something might be wrong. Telling herself that she would bury the poor things later, she made sure that they were all hidden behind the bushes, and then she turned and made her way back across the garden. She still felt as if she was being watched, and if anything that sensation had only grown over the previous few minutes; no matter how hard she tried to convince herself that she had to ignore the idea, finally she reached the gate at the side of the garden and felt almost as if someone or something was about to tap her shoulder from behind, as if -

"What?" she gasped, spinning around but seeing nobody at all.

Holding her breath for a moment, she once

again looked across the garden. Finally she sighed, furious at herself for being so easily spooked, and then she opened the gate and stepped out before she had a chance to allow herself any further indulgences. All she wanted, in that moment, was to get to the village and prove to her father that she was more than capable of conducting the family's business. Not that she was going to do things his way, of course. Indeed, she'd already come up with some improvements to his way of working that she felt sure would make everything easier.

Over on the other side of the lawn, the dead animals lay in the dirt. In the grass, meanwhile, thousands of ants lay beneath the green blades, where they'd been entirely missed by Lydia's eyes. And whereas just twenty-four hours earlier those ants had been swarming through their nest, now they were all dead, as were several dozen worms buried deeper beneath the ground.

CHAPTER EIGHT

"YOU'RE THOMAS SMITH'S GIRL, aren't you?" the woman in the shop said, eyeing Lydia skeptically while carrying a parcel of butter over to the counter. "I've not seen you since you were little, but I've got a good eye for these things."

"I am," Lydia replied politely. "My father sent me this morning to run a few errands."

"Is he not coming himself?"

"He's... busy," she explained, preferring to avoid going into too much detail. "Still, I rather think that the days are gone when the fairer sex can't be entrusted with a few small tasks. Don't you?"

She waited, but she could already tell that she'd said something wrong. The woman stared back at her for a moment, clearly unimpressed, before sliding the parcel toward her.

"Thank you," Lydia added.

"Your father isn't very picky," the woman said as she began to count the money. "He picks up any old rubbish from any old person, and he carts it off without even bothering to sort through it first."

"I believe that's part of his business," Lydia replied. "He takes everything, good and bad, and he disposes of it. Indeed, he can find a use for almost anything. That's one of his most valuable qualities."

"He should still be more discerning," the woman muttered. "There are some people whose belongings oughtn't to be kept by anyone. They ought to be burned."

"I'm sure I don't know what you mean," Lydia replied.

"It's none of my business, I'm sure," the woman said, fixing her with a dark stare. "I've just heard rumors, that's all. Old Mother Marston died a while back, and your father didn't waste any time arranging to take away her belongings, did he? Anything that the doctor and the priest didn't get their hands on first."

"My father isn't a thief," Lydia countered. "He always asks for -"

"I know that," the woman replied, interrupting her. "He gets permission before he takes anything. That's really not the point. The point is that sometimes people don't know what they're dealing with. I saw your father sorting through all sorts of things that had been thrown out of Old Mother Marston's cottage, and I thought to myself there and then that he ought to have more sense. Then again, he shouldn't have been given the chance in the first place. Somebody around here should have taken charge and burned the lot of it. In fact, if you ask me, someone should have burned the entire cottage down so that there was nothing left of it but a pile of ash."

"That seems a little... extreme," Lydia pointed out.

"Extreme's not always a bad thing," the woman said, rolling her eyes. "And how's your mother faring? I haven't seen her around for a while."

"She's... on the mend," Lydia explained diplomatically, knowing full well that her mother would never want to have her health discussed in public. "I'm sure she'll be much better soon."

"That's as well," the woman muttered as she started totting up the prices of the various items on the counter. "Mary's always seemed like a sensible woman to me. Once she's up on her feet, I'm sure she'll be sorting your father out and knocking some sense back into that head of his."

***

As she made her way across the village green, ready for the long walk back to the house, Lydia couldn't help but notice that a group of two dozen or so men had convened over by the large oak tree. She knew that the oak tree was used for important meetings, and she saw that while none of the village's womenfolk had been invited to join, several of the wives and daughters were loitering with earshot of whatever was going on.

Slowing her pace, Lydia made her way a little closer. She noticed the disapproving expressions on the faces of various women nearby, but she told herself that she had as much right as anyone to see what was happening.

"I told you all," a man at the front of the small crowd was saying as Lydia finally managed to hear, "we should have dealt with this matter earlier. There's no use waiting, not when it's obvious what needs doing. If we'd made our move at the right time, we'd be enjoying greater fortune now, that's for sure."

"And what would you suggest we should have done?" another man asked. "We haven't had a witch hunt round these parts in more than a hundred years."

"More's the pity," a third man suggested, leading to a general murmur of agreement from the crowd.

Lydia raised a surprised eyebrow.

"Listen up," another man added, stepping away from the others and then turning to address them all, "it seems to me that most of this conversation is entirely unnecessary. Yes, we could have done something, but you're all missing the fact that the old woman's dead now. She died of natural causes. Old age, call it whatever you want, but she's gone at last and we should be celebrating that fact."

"At last?" Lydia whispered. "That doesn't sound very friendly."

"What are you doing here?" one of the other girls asked, keeping her voice low as she looked Lydia up and down. Nearby, the men were still talking. "Shouldn't you be down on your knees in the mud somewhere?"

A few other girls began to laugh.

"What's going on?" Lydia asked.

"What business is it of yours?" the first girl snapped back. "You live on that ramshackle old farm, don't you?"

"I was just curious."

"Why?" the girl replied as a broad grin spread across her face. "Are you witches all sticking together?"

"Enough of that!" an older woman hissed, slapping the girl hard and pushing her away. "Esme Walker, you'll go home and get on with scrubbing the floor. I won't hear more from your wicked mouth!"

Clearly in pain, the girl looked to be almost in tears as she hurried away, leaving a somewhat puzzled Lydia trying to work out exactly what had just happened.

"Pay no mind to her," the older woman said, "she's seventeen years of age but sometimes she acts more like she's half that. In her head, at least." She paused for a moment. "You're the Smith girl, aren't you? You live in the old farmhouse a little way past the edge of the village."

"That's right," Lydia replied, before looking over at the men again. "I just wondered about the commotion, that's all."

"There's no commotion," the woman told her. "Not now, at least. The commotion, if there was ever one, ended last week when Old Mother Marston died. You ever heard of her?"

"I don't think so."

"Then keep it that way," the woman said firmly. "She was a dangerous woman, and she dabbled in dark arts. There wasn't a single person in this entire village who was happy about her living here, we all shunned her and rightly so. She must have been eighty if she was a day, but she's gone now and we've given her a good burial in hallowed ground. Hopefully that'll be the end of her evil."

"Was she really evil?" Lydia asked. "In what way?"

"That's none of your concern!" the woman

replied. "You'd do well to be on your way, so that your innocent little ears aren't sullied by talk of witchcraft. It's everyone's hope now that we can get on with things and forget Old Mother Marston ever existed. All that's left to do now is decide the fate of her cottage. There are some who think it should be torn down, but personally I think that'd be a shame. It's a good little home and the woman's dead now, so she can't hurt anyone. There's such a thing as too much superstition."

Lydia opened her mouth to reply, but for a moment she could only stare at the men as she realized that these villagers were serious: they actually believed that a witch had been living in their community, and despite her apparent death they were still worried that she might somehow be able to get at them. Although she was by no means worldly, Lydia couldn't help thinking that the people of Almsford seemed to be out of their minds.

"Be on your way," the woman said finally, before nudging Lydia's arm. "You don't know how lucky you are, living out there away from all this nonsense. Trust me, what you're seeing today is nothing compared to the foolishness these men get up to, and some of the women are even worse. The best thing for all of us is just to let them get it out of their minds." She leaned closer and lowered her voice to a whisper. "Even in these supposedly enlightened times, it doesn't do to attract too much attention. Remember that."

"I will," Lydia replied, before turning and starting to walk away. "Thank you."

After a few paces, she couldn't help but look over her shoulder, watching the men as they continued to talk. One man, a particularly handsome fellow around her own age, glanced at her briefly. Blushing, Lydia forced herself to turn away. She soon picked up her pace, and deep down she was already hoping that she'd have no reason to visit Almsford again at any point in the near future.

CHAPTER NINE

"I'M JUST LOOKING FOR a few things!" she called out a few hours later, kneeling in the storeroom at the back of the farmhouse. "I won't be long!"

"Alright, fair enough!" her father shouted back at her from the kitchen. "Just let me know when you're done!"

"I will," she muttered, but already she'd turned her attention back to the box she'd just pulled away from the wall. "Don't you worry about that."

Having searched for a while, she realized that she'd finally located the last box of books her father had brought from the village recently. She knew that these books represented a collection from various houses, but she reasoned that at least some of them had to be similar to the one she'd found earlier; sure enough, she quickly found several books featuring the same squirrely text and strange images, and she immediately felt herself drawn into what seemed to be various unusual rhymes and poems.

"If gold you seek," she whispered, reading out loud from one of the pages, "you'll find it where... there's blood and flesh and locks of hair."

She turned to the next page.

"Be sure to hold this secret tight," she continued, "or all your gold will -"

Suddenly hearing a bumping sound, she turned and looked at some shelves in the corner of the room. She told herself that the sound was most likely caused by nothing at all, yet the disturbance persisted and she quickly realized that something was lurking behind the various rotten old bags and boxes; worried that some more rats might have found their way into the house, she set the book aside and got to her feet, before grabbing a broom and hurrying over to the corner.

"You're not welcome here," she said, using her foot to move some of the bags aside, and immediately hearing the scratching sound again as something scurried out of sight. "We don't want vermin in this house!"

She pulled some more bags out of the way, and then she knelt again and peered past a few of the boxes. As she waited, she realized that the sound had stopped; she wasn't sure that rats were clever enough to hide for very long, but as she looked into the shadows beyond the boxes she couldn't help but feel as if something was staring back out at her. Feeling more than a little unnerved, she moved a couple of the boxes aside, but to her surprise she saw nothing lurking further back in the darkness. A moment later she looked at the side of the nearest box and saw that the name Smythe had been painted on the wood, which meant that these particular boxes probably came from the old Smythe farm at the other edge of the village. That place had been good pickings for her father over the years, ever since it had been left abandoned.

"You're lucky this time," she muttered, getting to her feet as she realized that the rat – or whatever it might have been – had clearly managed to elude her. "If we cross paths again, I'll have to finish you off fast."

As she picked up the old books and headed out of the storeroom, she had no idea that two dark, beady eyes were watching her from behind some of the boxes in the farthest corner.

***

"Mother, you should try to eat *something*," Lydia said that evening, as she sat next to her mother on the bed upstairs. "You'll feel a lot better if -"

"Don't tell me what to do!" Mary hissed angrily, trying but failing to sit up in the bed, causing the entire wooden frame to creak and groan loudly. "You're a child!"

"I know that," Lydia said patiently, "but I only have your best interests at heart. Mother, I want nothing more than to see you rise from here and get on with your daily work, so -"

"Oh, so now you're lazy, are you?" Mary muttered, reaching over toward the little table next to the bed. "You tire of your work and you can't wait for me to take over again. That really shouldn't surprise me, should it? You've always been a pitiful little wretch and -"

Before she could get another word out, she knocked a glass from the table, sending it crashing down until it smashed against the floor.

"Curse you!" she snapped angrily. "Look what you've made me do!"

"I'll clear it up," Lydia replied, getting to her feet and heading to the dresser, where she grabbed a bowl and then carried it back over. "Don't strain yourself. I can do this."

"I'm not a cripple!" Mary hissed, already leaning over the side of the bed and starting to pick up the glass shards. "I'm still your mother, and you'd do well to remember that fact!"

"Of course I remember it," Lydia said, kneeling to help. "How could I ever forget such a precious and sacred thing? Why can't you understand that I merely wish to help you and -"

"Leave me alone!" Mary shrieked, slashing a broken glass shard across the girl's face, causing her to pull back with a cry of pain. "I'm not an invalid!"

Too shocked to know how to react, Lydia scrambled across the room until her back was against the wall. Reaching up, she touched the side of her face and felt hot blood dribbling down from a cut on her cheek; the glass had sliced a wound several inches long, just below her eye, and for a few seconds Lydia simply couldn't believe that something so awful had happened. As she watched her mother trying furiously to clean up the mess, she felt more blood running from the cut on her cheek until finally she realized that she must be responsible for such an awful incident. After all, she knew her mother would never have lashed out like that without provocation.

"I'm sorry," Lydia murmured, with tears filling her eyes as she stumbled to her feet. "Forgive me, Mother, I should have listened to you."

"Stupid little whore!" Mary sneered, trying to gather up the other glass pieces but succeeding only in pushing most of them under the bed. "Your father and I always wanted a boy! What are we supposed to do with someone as weak and pathetic as you?"

"I'm sorry," Lydia said again, before hurrying from the room and then stopping to weep in the corridor.

Putting her hands over her face, she tried to get her emotions under control, yet all she could think was that yet again she'd failed her parents. A moment later, hearing another door creaking open, she tried to sniff back the tears as she turned to see her father stepping out from the other bedroom.

"I heard a commotion," he said sternly.

"It's nothing."

"It sounded like something."

"Mother's just... upset, that's all," Lydia explained, wiping away tears but inadvertently smearing blood across her face. "It's my fault."

"No doubt," Thomas murmured, staring at her for a moment as if deep in thought. "Your mother needs her rest. You shouldn't disturb her."

"I know. I'm sorry."

"You'll sleep in here with me tonight," he continued. "It's going to be a cold one and I shall need the warmth of another body."

"Are..."

Her voice trailed off for a moment.

"Are you sure?" she asked, feeling a growing sense of dread rising through her chest. She always hated the nights when her father requested her company. "I'm so very tired and -"

"You'll sleep in here with me tonight," he

said again, pushing the door further open so that she could be in no doubt. "You wouldn't deny me that, would you? You're my daughter, and with your mother in her present condition, you have a duty to take her place." He paused again. "In all possible ways."

She wanted to scream, but deep down Lydia knew that there was no way to change his mind. Sometimes she could get him so drunk that he'd merely fall asleep, yet there was no time for that now and she knew that she was simply going to have to acquiesce to his every need. At least the nights never lasted too long, and he seemed to not mind if she subsequently retired to some other spot in the house; so long as he was satisfied, she supposed that she would be able to escape soon enough, at least until the next time.

"Are you delaying?" he asked.

"No," she replied, as she heard her mother sobbing and muttering in the other bedroom. "I must just wash my face first, though. You will allow me to do that, will you not?"

"Don't take too long," he said darkly, keeping his gaze fixed on her. "I've waited all evening and it would be unfair to make me wait any longer. And don't forget to shut the door to your mother's room. The last thing I need is to hear her hollering and howling later."

With that, he stepped back into the master

bedroom. Lydia hesitated for a moment before reaching out to pull the other door shut.

"Good luck," she heard her mother whispering bitterly, her tone mixed with a hint of mocking laughter. "Try not to disturb me with your wretched screams."

CHAPTER TEN

SEVERAL HOURS LATER, SITTING on the floor in the cold storeroom, Lydia sniffed back more tears. She was trying hard to forget everything that had happened in the bedroom, but brief jarring glimpses kept breaking through even as she squeezed her eyes tight shut. Digging her fingernails deep into her palms, she tried to conjure up enough pain to block out the memory of her own cries.

"You're cold," she heard her father's voice complaining, echoing through her thoughts. "Why is your skin so cold?"

She remembered the sound of the bed creaking, and the sensation of the wooden slats bending and almost breaking beneath her back. She knew such thoughts were wicked, yet she couldn't help wishing that those slats might have snapped and forced their broken ends straight up, ripping through her chest and killing her instantly. Wiping away more tears, she told herself that she had to be a better person, and she tried to focus on the fact that her father was sick and needed help. And with her mother still bed-bound, she was the only -

Suddenly she heard a scratching sound, coming from somewhere behind the boxes on the far side of the room.

Immediately concerned that more rats had entered the house, she sat up a little. In some dark way, she was relieved to have the rats to focus on; at least this would give her something else to think about, so after a moment she got to her feet and grabbed the broom from nearby. Still sniffing back tears, she was nevertheless able to put all other thoughts out of her mind as she began to approach the boxes; hitting scurrying rats with a broom was usually difficult, but she'd had a few successes in the past and she was determined to try again. Already she could hear the scratching sound continuing, coming from behind one of the larger Smythe Farm boxes. Stopping for a moment, she adjusted her grip on the broom and held her breath, preparing to strike.

In an instant, she kicked the box aside and saw a dark shape flashing past. Slamming the broom down, she hit the fleeing creature and knocked it hard, sending it smashing into the wall. Hoping that its senses might be dulled, she hit it again, and she heard a faint crying sound as the beast hit the wall opposite. Shocked by the size of this rat, Lydia channeled all her rage and anger into her hands, turning the broom and hitting the creature for a third time, then raising the handle and preparing to bring it crashing down with enough force to kill what appeared to be a rather large rat.

And then, at the very last second, as she was about to deliver the death blow she saw that this was not a rat at all.

Instead, cowering in the corner, a black cat stared back up at her with terrified eyes. Lydia froze, still holding the broom up as if she meant to strike, but finally she sighed as she heard the cat let out a pitiful mewling sound.

"What are you doing in here?" she asked, setting the broom aside and getting down onto her knees. She reached for the cat, only to see it recoil in fear. "It's alright," she continued, "I'm not going to hurt you. I thought you were something else, that's all."

The cat pulled further away, clearly terrified, and Lydia could see now that the poor thing was in a terrible state. Weak and ragged, with patches of bare skin where its fur was gone, the cat appeared to be utterly starved. Indeed, a moment later the animal tried to stand, struggling to control its back legs, and its tail was little more than a matted cord dangling loose from the back of its body. Lydia had never seen such a wretched sight in her life, and she could only assume that the cat must have been starving to death in the storeroom for quite some time.

"You poor thing," she whispered after a moment. "You must be so scared."

She instinctively reached out again, and this time the cat turned and limped away, slipping behind the Smythe Farm box and disappearing from sight. Lydia waited, but she could hear a repetitive bumping sound, and she realized that the cat seemed to be shivering with fear or hunger – or perhaps both.

"This is no good," she muttered, getting to her feet and hurrying into the kitchen, where she found some of the bread and cheese she'd been saving for the morning.

Once she'd cut the food up, she carried it back into the storeroom and set it down on the floor. She waited, but the cat showed no sign that it was brave enough yet to come out; worried that the animal might be mere hours from death, Lydia finally reached over and moved the box aside, and then she slid the plate a little closer.

"It's good food," she said, seeing that the cat was once again backing away. "I'm so sorry that I hit you with that broom, and that I tried to... Well, I thought you were a rat, that's all. And to be fair, you're really not *that* much larger than a rat, are you?"

She peered a little closer, before pulling back as she realized that she might well frighten the poor cat to death.

"I'm friendly," she continued. "Actually, even though you might find that difficult to believe, I assure you that I mean you no harm whatsoever, but I'm afraid I can't say the same for my parents. My mother has a history with cats, although she's confined to bed so I don't think she'll be able to do you any harm at present. My father might be more disposed to you, so long as you keep out of his way." She thought for a moment. "All in all, I think it might be better if you stay hidden. Do you think you can do that?"

She slid the plate closer, but the bottom scraped against the floor and this sound clearly scared the cat further.

"I'm sorry," Lydia said, pulling her hand back, "it seems as if everything I do is wrong."

She thought again, trying to think of some way to make it all right.

"I don't know how you got in here," she continued, smiling as she saw the two terrified dark eyes glaring back up at her, "but you're clearly in need of help. You must let me clean you up, at the very least, and try to fatten you up as well. You probably won't like this very much, but I rather think that I'm going to have to take control. You'll be glad after the fact."

With that, she moved the box aside and reached for the cat. This time, when the animal recoiled once more, Lydia insisted on taking hold of its scrawny body and lifting it up. She heard a loud hissing sound and saw the cat open its mouth, bearing its fangs, but as she held the animal aloft and got to her feet she told herself that she could no longer be deterred.

"I'm going to help you," she said firmly as the cat wriggled violently in her hands. She could almost feel bones jutting out from beneath the fur. "You have to understand that I -"

Suddenly she gasped as the cat bit her left hand, sinking its teeth deep into the flesh around the base of her thumb. Letting out a pained cry, Lydia let go of the animal and stepped back. The cat dropped down, landing on its feet and quickly scrambling back behind the box, and Lydia was left to look down at her hand and watch as blood dribbled from the holes left by the fangs.

"I was trying to help you!" she hissed, taking a handkerchief from her pocket and wiping some of the blood away. "Are you so fearful that you can't separate friend from foe?"

She wiped off more blood, and then she looked at the corner and saw that the cat had once again disappeared behind the box. Sighing, she realized that the poor thing was clearly almost beyond help; part of her wanted to try again to pick it up, to use a little extra caution this time, but after a few seconds she realized that the best approach might simply be to let the animal have more time. She used her right foot to slide the plate closer to the side of the box, but still there was no sign of the cat emerging to feed.

"It's there if you decide you want it," she explained, wincing as she felt the bite on her hand still stinging. "I hope you will, but I suppose I can't force you. Perhaps you're beyond help. Life can be like that sometimes, a soul can simply be too badly hurt to go on living." She paused as a shudder passed through her chest. "I hope dearly that you don't feel that way, but I think I've done all that I can."

Stepping back, she swallowed hard as she imagined the poor, terrified cat still shivering in the dark space behind the box.

"I hope you find the strength to carry on," she added. "It can be hard, sometimes. I know that full well myself. One can lose sight of any happiness ever coming again, but you must trust that the Lord will find a path for you. Oh, I don't know if it's wrong of me to speak of the Lord, you're just a wild animal and I'm sure you have no awareness of such things. Still, you're a living creature and you're part of God's world, so I suppose there must be some purpose for you."

She waited, almost as if she expected to hear an answer, and then she turned and headed to the door. Picking up her candle, she stepped out of the room and then turned to look back into the darkness; the plate of food lay on the floor still, untouched. For a few seconds Lydia tried to think of some way to help the cat, before finally realizing that perhaps all she could do was leave it alone and hope for the best. With that thought in mind, she gently bumped the door shut and wiped more blood from her hand as she began to limp toward the stairs.

CHAPTER ELEVEN

THE FOLLOWING MORNING, AS soon as she gently pushed the storeroom door open, Lydia saw that the plate remained on the floor with the bread and cheese still uneaten. The cat hadn't accepted the offered help, and indeed there was no sign of life at all. Had the poor thing already starved to death?

"What are you doing there?"

Startled, Lydia turned to see her father stepping into the hallway, still in the process of getting his arms into the sleeves of his shirt.

"Nothing," she stammered.

"You're doing something," he replied angrily.

"No, really," she said as he made his way over. "I'm sorry, I know I have other duties, I just -"

Before she could finish, Thomas pushed

past her and shoved the door open, marching into the storeroom and stopping for a moment to look around. Spotting the plate on the floor, he picked it up and turned to Lydia.

"What's this about?"

"Nothing."

"There's that word again," he replied, clearly suspicious already. "*Nothing*. I know when you're lying to me. Girl, nothing's nothing, not in the eyes of the Lord."

"I was trying to catch a particularly large... rat," she lied.

"A rat? Why?"

"It's been causing terrible trouble." She held up her hand, revealing the bite marks that were very slowly starting to crust over and heal. "It bit me last night."

"A rat bit you?"

She nodded, while glancing over at the Smythe Farm box and hoping very much that the cat would remain hidden. She could sense that her father was in the mood for blood.

"Must've been a hell of a rat," Thomas said after a few seconds, carrying the plate back out of the room. "You didn't poison any of this perfectly good food, did you?"

She shook her head.

"That's something, at least," he added, before shoving all the bread and cheese into his mouth, then handing the plate to his daughter. "My back's feeling better this morning and I'm sick of sitting around like some kind of simpleton. I'm going to clean out the space at the far end of the yard, and then tomorrow I'll be going into town." He walked back across the hallway. "I won't listen to any nonsense about resting, either. Not this time. Oh, and I heard your mother groaning about something upstairs. I don't know what's wrong, but she sounded particularly feeble. Go and check on her at some point."

"Of course," Lydia replied, waiting until he was gone before looking into the room again. She still saw no sign of the cat, and now she worried that it might have been scared away entirely.

A moment later, hearing a banging sound upstairs, she looked toward the staircase and realized that her father had been right about one thing: her mother was awake and was clearly in some kind of distress.

***

"It's not fine!" Mary hissed angrily, pushing Lydia away again as she once more tried to climb out of the bed. "Stop saying that all the time! Nothing about this is fine!"

"I don't think you should get up," Lydia replied, trying not to panic as the bed heaved and creaked and almost collapsed. She felt as if she'd had this exact same encounter with her mother a thousand times by now. "Mother, please, just -"

"You're nothing but your father's filth!" Mary snarled angrily, rolling onto her side once again. "You're a little -"

In that moment, the momentum of her roll proved too much. With a startled gasp, she tumbled over the side of the bed and landed with a heavy thud on the floor, bringing a trailing collection of stained sheets falling down after her and revealing a large hole that had been eaten away in the mattress itself.

"Help me!" she shouted frantically. "What are you doing to me? Help me up!"

"Mother, I did tell you not to try this," Lydia replied, stepping around her and trying to work out how to lift her off the floor. "You must learn to listen to me."

"Get me up!" Mary snapped. "You'll go to Hell for the way you treat me!"

"I'm going to lift you up right now," Lydia said, taking hold of her mother's arms and preparing to heave, telling herself that somehow she was going to manage the effort. "Don't fight me, okay? Try to assist me if you can."

"Hurry up!"

"Here we go," Lydia continued. "In three... two... one."

She took a deep breath, and then she began to try dragging her mother back up onto the bed. To her surprise, she was fairly quickly able to sit her on the side; although Mary was struggling and almost working against her, Lydia nevertheless propped her onto the bed's edge, and then she tried to tilt her around so that she could settle her against the pillows. She had to adjust her grip and move around slightly. Her arms were aching and she could feel a tightening pain in the small of her back, but she supposed that with just one last pull she might -

"Enough!" Mary roared, pushing Lydia back and sending her falling down. "I can do the rest! I want dignity!"

Landing hard, Lydia let out a gasp as she felt the pain in her back twist and tighten. She immediately tried to get up, but some part of her lower back felt as if it had almost locked tight. The effort of rising proved far too much, and after a few more attempts she could only just about manage to get onto her knees. Telling herself that the pain in her back would subside at any moment, as it had always done in the past, she waited; this time, however, something felt a little different, and when she tried again to stand she immediately winced.

"What's wrong with you?" Mary sneered.

"Nothing," Lydia replied, still hopeful that the pain wouldn't prove permanent.

"Then what are you still doing down there?

You're nothing but a lazy little wretch!"

"I'm sorry," Lydia said, determined to wait a few more seconds. "Just give me one moment and I'll be up again."

"You're young," her mother purred, her voice positively dripping with jealousy. "You've got no excuses for weakness. You're not like me, mercilessly abused and treated like some kind of old fool." She began to roll herself back onto her other side, although she was clearly struggling to move at all. "I only wanted to get up and go outside, that's all. Do you know how long it's been since I got a breath of fresh air? But I suppose that's too much to ask, I'm to be confined in this room for the rest of my life. Sometimes I think you and your father are engaged in some kind of plot to finish me off."

"Nothing could be further from the truth," Lydia told her. "We're trying to help you get back on your feet. If you'd just listen and -"

"Nobody listens to *me*!" Mary complained angrily. "I might as well talk to myself!"

Lydia was about to reply when she saw her mother's tattered nightshirt lifting slightly at the rear, revealing mottled grayish-blue skin that appeared to be in the process of rotting. There were holes in the flesh, too, almost as if something had been burrowing into her mother's body.

"Wait," Lydia said, "your back looks -"

"Leave me alone!" Mary shouted, finally

giving up on any attempt to turn and instead slumping back down against the pillows. "Just leave me to wallow up here. That way, you and your father can get on with whatever you do to occupy your time. Don't think I don't hear you getting up to all sorts of things in the rest of the house. I'm not surprised you want to keep me confined in here like some kind of common prisoner. I bet even in the Tower of London, the most wretched of the condemned are given better conditions."

She looked Lydia up and down for a moment, scrunching her nose to show her discontent.

"I can smell him on you," she sneered finally.

"That is not the case," Lydia replied, before forcing herself up. The pain in her back rippled again, almost dragging her back down, but she somehow managed to stagger across the room so that she could lean against the door. "I'm sorry, I've pulled something in my back, I just need to straighten it out a little and then I'll make you some breakfast. I'll be up again as quickly as I can manage."

As soon as she was out in the corridor, Lydia leaned back against the wall and clenched her teeth. The pain in her back was getting worse, but she knew she couldn't stop working. Instead, she told herself that she simply had to push through any discomfort. She could only hope that eventually her back would fix itself. To that end, she turned and made her way toward the top of the stairs, although she had to stop again for a few seconds to brace herself for the agony she knew she'd feel when she started to make her way down.

CHAPTER TWELVE

SEVERAL HOURS LATER, AS she limped across the kitchen, Lydia felt another twisting surge of pain in her back. She stopped and waited for the worst to pass, but she was already fairly sure that the damage to her spine was more severe than she'd initially assumed. Still, there were chores to complete, so she forced herself to head over to the cupboard in the far corner of the room.

Reaching inside, she hesitated for a moment, worried that rats might attack her. When she heard no sign of movement at all, she moved some of the old jars out of the way and saw to her surprise that – perhaps for the first time ever – there was no sign of any rats at all. She'd cleaned the cupboards as usual that morning, getting rid of any feces pellets, but she knew from bitter experience that the rats always dropped more on an almost hourly basis. This time, however, there were none to be seen at all.

Indeed, as she peered into the cupboard for a few more seconds, Lydia realized that something else had changed in the house. She looked all around, and she noted that the usual scrabbling and scratching sound of the rats' little claws was gone; she waited for some hint of movement behind the walls or perhaps high above in the ceiling, yet no such sound emerged. She knew that the rats couldn't simply have vanished, yet she had to admit that they certainly seemed to have been quieted by something. The longer she waited for some sign of their presence, the more confused she felt by the fact that they seemed to have entirely gone.

"How curious," she whispered under her breath, before taking two of the jars and setting them on the counter.

Looking out the window, she saw her father working at the far end of the yard. She watched him for a moment, relieved that he was busy and hopeful that he'd soon tire himself out. She knew full well that he was only really a danger in the evenings if he'd been less busy during the day; she much preferred the nights when he retired early to bed, because then she knew she'd be left alone. Now she waited until he walked out of sight, and then she turned and headed through to the storeroom, making a mental note of all the items she needed to collect.

And then, as she pushed the door open and looked into the room, she froze as she found herself confronted by the most astonishing sight.

The entire floor of the storeroom was covered in dead rats, which had been laid out in a remarkably organized grid pattern. As she looked around at so many corpses – there were at least seventy or eighty rats before her, perhaps as many as a hundred – Lydia saw that they'd all been left fairly intact, although blood had dribbled out from some of them. Having been in the storeroom just an hour or so earlier, Lydia knew that these rats had to have been put in place very recently, although she had no idea why her father would ever have done such a thing.

A moment later she heard a shuffling sound, and she looked across the room just in time to see the black cat watching her from behind the Smythe Farm box.

"Did *you* do this?" she asked, furrowing her brow. "But... how? And when? I don't understand."

She hesitated, before venturing into the room. Taking care to avoid stepping on any of the corpses, she picked her way over to the box, although she stopped when she saw the cat starting to pull back out of sight.

"No, wait!" she said. "Don't go!"

The cat stopped, still just about in view for a few seconds before stepping forward again. This time, its black tail curled slowly as it moved.

"It *is* you, isn't it?" Lydia said. "You look so much better than last night. I'm almost tempted to think that you're a different cat altogether, except... I can see that it's definitely you. There's a rather distinctive quality in your eyes."

She paused, and then she crouched down. To her astonishment, the cat began to make its way forward, and this time the animal didn't pull away when Lydia reached out with a hand. She stroked its side and immediately noticed that its fur was much softer than before. In fact, the animal had undergone an overnight transformation that seemed scarcely believable, and she couldn't help but wonder how any creature could have recovered its health so quickly. Whereas around twelve hours earlier this cat had appeared to be on the verge of death, now it was evidently doing extremely well. Although she was by no means an expert in such things, Lydia still felt sure that such a rapid improvement had to be almost impossible.

"You look familiar," she continued after a few seconds, tilting her head slightly. "I know how strange this will sound, but I'm sure I've seen you before. I don't just mean last night, I mean a long time ago. I'm just struggling to place where and when."

She thought for a moment, puzzled by the sense of deja vu until finally a very strange and implausible idea bubbled up to the surface of her mind.

"Wait," she said softly, "there's no conceivable way you could possibly be -"

"What's going on in here?" Thomas barked, pushing the door open and stepping into the room, immediately crushing two of the rat corpses beneath his hefty right boot. "What the hell is all this?"

"Father, don't be angry!" Lydia gasped, getting to her feet and turning to him. "I know it must seem -"

In that moment he struck her across the face, sending her crashing back down. She landed hard on the corpses, and the black cat scrambled away to hide behind the box.

"This place is filthy!" Thomas snapped, storming past Lydia and grabbing the box, hauling it up and throwing it so hard that it smashed against the far wall.

The black cat raced out from the corner and tried to get away, only for Thomas to kick it in the side. Crying out, the cat was sent flying across the room until it slammed into the wall, although it managed to land on its feet and quickly hurried out of the room.

"What in the name of all that's holy is going on in this madhouse?" Thomas shouted angrily, before looking down to see that Lydia was slowly sitting up. He paused, short of breath, before grabbing her arm and hauling her up onto her feet. "I've seen some strange things in my time," he continued, "but this just about beats them all."

"I'm sorry," Lydia sobbed, with one side of her face already reddened from the strike. "I just came in a moment ago and found it all like this."

"You knew nothing about a cat skulking around?"

"I saw him last night and -"

"So you've known since last night?" he hissed, before letting go of her arm and stepping back, crunching a few more dead rats under his boots in the process. Looking around, he seemed utterly shocked by the sight. "Ignoring the deception for a moment," he muttered, "I suppose the filthy thing seems to have done a good job. We've long been plagued by rats on this farm."

"Does that mean we can keep him?" Lydia asked.

He turned and scowled at her.

"I *think* he's male, anyway," she continued. "Father, I was going to tell you about him, I promise. It's just that everything has happened so quickly and I wasn't even sure what to believe."

"I've said it before and I'll say it again," Thomas replied, "if a cat can pay its own way around here, and if it's intelligent enough to keep out of my way, then it shall be tolerated. Not as a pet, but as a working animal."

"I'll look after him," she promised. "You'll barely even know that he's here at all."

"I don't want you going soft on me," he murmured darkly, looking deep into her tear-filled eyes as if he still wasn't entirely convinced, "and I don't want you wasting time fussing over the thing. Any duties relating to the cat are to be conducted in your own time, is that clear?"

"Of course."

"And you're to keep it out from under my feet."

"I will, I promise."

"And don't give me any reason to regret my kindness in this matter," he added, before reaching up and using a thumb to wipe away a tear from her cheek. "I'm sorry I struck you, Lydia. I shouldn't have done that, but my anger got the better of me and the pain in my back... I know you don't understand what that's like, but sometimes I fear it's driving me out of my mind."

"I know you're a good man, Father," she told him.

"And you're a good daughter," he said, wiping away another of her tears. "The best a man could ever hope for, if I'm honest." He paused, staring deep into her eyes before stepping back. "I need you to come into the village with me this afternoon after all."

"But -"

"No arguments," he added. "I have to get on with things, but I need help with one or two matters. You'll tend to your duties here and then be ready to come with me one hour from now. And don't tell your mother that I struck you, Lydia. You know how much she nags, and I don't want her to have any cause to complain about anything." He looked down at the dead rats. "And clean these filthy things up. I truly can't stand the sight of them."

CHAPTER THIRTEEN

THE GLASS IN THE window broke a little louder than she'd expected. Turning, Lydia looked back across the yard, but she saw nothing to indicate that anyone else had heard.

"Are you sure we should be doing this?" she whispered, as her father reached through the broken window and fiddled with the lock.

"I heard rumors that there's more worth having in this cottage," Thomas muttered, before pushing the door open and stepping into the dark little back room. "The old woman didn't have any family, so it's not as if I'll be depriving anyone of anything, is it? The folks who cleared out the place probably missed all sorts of valuables. If you think about it, I'm actually going to be doing the fair people of Almsford a favor."

"I suppose that's one way of thinking about it," Lydia replied, hurrying after him, keen to get out of sight. "Wouldn't anything worth taking have already been left outside, though?"

"There's no harm in making sure," he said firmly as he moved through into the front room. Stopping for a moment, silhouetted against the blinding light streaming through the front window, he looked around. "Mind you, the place certainly looks empty. I don't think this'll take long."

"I hope not," Lydia replied.

"I'll check down here," he continued, "and you can go upstairs. Old Mother Marston seems to have been one of those types who never let go of much. Occasionally people like that can squirrel away something valuable, so make sure you search in all the nooks and crannies." He paused, before turning to his daughter. "Well? What are you waiting for? Get up there and take a look around!"

***

"This place is utterly filthy," Lydia said under her breath a few minutes later, stepping over some piles of old clothes that had been left on the floor of the front bedroom. The wooden boards bent a little beneath her steps. "How could anyone live in such a manner?"

Stopping to look at the bed, she winced as

she saw a dark brown stain that seemed to approximate the shape of a human. Although she knew next to nothing about this Old Mother Marston woman, or about the circumstances of her life, Lydia had come to the conclusion that the old woman must have spent her final years living alone in the most dreadful conditions. Every room in the house was moldy and damp, with plenty of spiders having made thick webs in the high corners. Rat droppings had been left all over the place, and even now Lydia could see that the bed-sheets had been gnawed by tiny mouths.

"She could have done with a cat," she whispered.

Worse, though, was the almost unbearable stench. Part of the mattress was stained a darker, deeper shade of brown, and Lydia could tell that the old woman must have soiled herself regularly. Picking her way around the bed, she looked down at the floor on the other side and immediately recoiled as she saw several old pots of dark – perhaps even bloodied – urine. Almost throwing up, Lydia hurried back to the door and paused for a moment to try to pull herself together. The floor creaked beneath her weight again, but after a few seconds she was able to start ignoring the smell at least a little.

"Well?" Thomas called up from downstairs. "Did you find anything?"

"Nothing worth taking," she replied.

"Father, there's nothing here but foul old sheets. I think we're wasting our time."

"I'll be the judge of that. I heard you in the front bedroom, but what about the one at the back?"

"Father -"

"We're here now," he added. "We're going to make sure."

"Indeed," she said with a sigh, before taking as deep a breath as she dared in such a noxious environment. "I think -"

"Go no further."

Startled, she spun around and looked back at the bed. The voice had been old and gnarled, as if it had crawled from a dry and almost closed throat. Staring at the bed now, Lydia felt sure that she'd heard an old woman speaking from that exact spot, yet now she saw once more that the bed was empty. She looked around, worried that she might have company, yet she knew deep down that she was all alone in the room.

"Hello?" she whispered, not wanting to alert her father, who she knew would only chide her for foolishness. "Is... is anyone there?"

She waited, and although the room remained still and silent she couldn't shake the feeling that she was somehow being watched. After a few seconds she found herself wondering whether the remains of the mattress appeared to have sunk a little, almost as if – since she'd entered the room – the weight of a person had begun to press down.

"Is there anyone in here?" she asked again, still keeping her voice low.

Again she waited, and now she could feel cold sweat breaking out across her face. Finally, resolving to bring herself to her senses, she turned to head out onto the landing.

"Go no further," the voice croaked again, and this time Lydia froze in the doorway. She heard the unmistakable sound of the bed's fragile wooden frame shifting. "Let it be."

Slowly, Lydia turned and looked back at the bed. She still saw no sign of anyone, yet now more than ever she felt sure that there was another presence in the room.

"Let me see you," she said softly. "Show me that someone's really here."

The room remained defiantly bare, yet Lydia felt sure that if she turned her back on the bed she'd hear the voice again. After a few more seconds, wondering whether this might in fact be the only way to communicate with whoever lingered in the room, she forced herself to turn away, and she almost immediately heard the bed creaking once more.

"Who are you?" she whispered. "Are you the old woman who used to live here?"

This time she heard no reply, although a moment later her father could be heard roughly sorting through some items in the room below.

"Are you still here somehow?" Lydia asked, imagining the old woman watching her from the bed. "I'm not afraid. Well, I suppose I am, but if you're here then I should very much like to see you. I should like to know if such things are possible. If I turn around, do you promise that you'll let me see you? I won't scream or make any kind of commotion."

She swallowed hard, and then she slowly turned and looked at the bed.

Nothing.

The room remained empty, and already Lydia was starting to wonder whether she might have imagined the whole thing. She waited for a few seconds, but already any sense of a gaze seemed to be fading away, leaving her standing all alone.

"Are you done up there?" her father shouted suddenly. "Did the old fool leave anything useful behind?"

"Nothing," Lydia replied, watching the bed for a moment longer before turning and heading toward the top of the stairs. "I'm afraid there's nothing to -"

Before she could take another step, her left foot broke through a loose board on the floor. Startled, she let out a gasp of pain as she steadied herself against the wall. Looking down, she saw that she'd cracked one particular floorboard, revealing what appeared to be a narrow space below. She almost ignored the damage, but after a moment she crouched down and peered at some kind of object that had been left hidden in the gap. Reaching inside, she had to shift the object a few times, before finally pulling out a very old, very stained leather-bound book. Astonished by her discovery, she opened the book and saw that it contained page after page of handwritten notes, although many of the pages were discolored by what appeared to be faded patches of blood.

Transfixed by the notes, and by the drawings she found on some pages, Lydia continued to leaf through the book. She could already tell that this was written by the same hand as the items her father had discovered previously, yet these appeared to be much more complete. Despite a slight pain in the back of her head as she studied the book, she was unable to tear her attention away, and finally she realized she could feel her blood rushing hard and her heart pounding frantically in her chest. A moment later a bead of saliva escaped from one corner of her mouth and dribbled down her chin.

"Well?"

Broken out of her spell, Lydia turned and fell back, landing hard on the floor. She could see her father's shadow on the wall at the bottom of the staircase.

"Why didn't you answer me?" he barked. "I've been calling you. Are you done up there or not?"

"I am, Father," she stammered, relieved that he hadn't made his way up and seen the book. "There's nothing. If you don't believe me, come and see for yourself."

"There's no need for that," he sighed. "I'm going to go and look at some scrap at the end of the alley. I'll meet you out near the back of the cottage in a few minutes. Make sure no-one sees you loitering."

CHAPTER FOURTEEN

SITTING ON THE GRASS in the alley that ran past the rear of the cottage, Lydia found herself once again flicking through the pages of the book. She knew she should be more careful, that she should hide it all away until she reached home, but something about the text and images seemed to be demanding her attention, almost as if she couldn't possibly *ever* look away again.

"You're so beautiful," she whispered, running a hand across one of the mottled pages, not even minding the stained blood. "And old. So old that -"

Before she could finish, she heard footsteps approaching. Panicking at the thought of her father seeing her with the book, she quickly hid it behind her back and got to her feet, but as she turned she saw that a different man was making his way along the alley. She knew she recognized him, but it was only as he got closer that she realized he was the same man she'd seen a few days earlier speaking in the village about the dangers of witchcraft.

"Good morning," he said, eyeing her with a hint of suspicion as he stopped just a few feet away. Now that he was closer, he seemed younger than she'd realized and a lot more handsome. "What brings a fair young lady out all alone in the middle of the day like this?"

"I'm waiting for my father," she replied, keeping the book hidden behind her back. "He'll be here soon."

"He will, will he?" the man said, smiling slightly as he looked both ways along the alley. "I haven't seen anyone else around."

"He's only looking for scrap," she explained. "For things that others have discarded. He's not breaking any laws."

"I never for one moment suggested such a thing," the man replied, turning to her for a moment before looking at the rear of Old Mother Marston's cottage. "You've chosen an odd place to stop. There's nothing good that could ever come from spending too long in this part of the village."

"I'm sure I don't know what you mean," she told him.

"Come," he said, stepping closer and

reaching out to take her hand, "let me take you around to the front. You'll be happier there."

Not wanting to agree, but also unwilling to cause a fuss, Lydia quickly realized that she had no choice. She let the man link his arm through hers, and she begrudgingly allowed him to lead her back along the alley. Although she hated being touched, she tried to hide that fact from the stranger.

"I've seen you before," he told her. "I believe you passed by the other day while I was speaking. I'm sorry if that makes you feel awkward, but I remember noticing your beauty."

"You're too kind," she said, trying not to blush.

"It's rare to see fresh beauty round these parts," he continued. "Do you live in Almsford or are you just visiting?"

"We live a little way out of the village," she explained. "Do you know Bloodacre Farm?"

"I have heard of it," he admitted. "Not the most cheerful name, but so long as the land is good, I suppose that's all that matters. I understand that crops have been poor for a few years around these parts. There are some who argue that this is punishment from above for the fact that our village has been harboring evil."

"Evil?"

"But I'm sure you don't know anything about that," he continued, leading her around to the front of the cottage before pulling his arm away and taking a step back. He conspicuously looked her up and down for a moment. "If you heed my advice, you'll focus only on good, pious thoughts. You seem like a sweet, innocent and faithful young lady, but such qualities can easily become poisoned by the darker elements that persist in this world. Sometimes it can be hard to recognize those elements until it's too late. Tell me, do you go to church?"

"It can be hard to get there," she admitted, "but we certainly pray."

"You should make the effort," he said firmly. "I imagine that from your farm, it would take quite some time to reach St. Margaret's, but you would be more than amply rewarded. Myself, I walk there and back every Sunday. The journey takes two hours each way, but I'm always glad of the chance for some silent contemplation, and sometimes I meet strangers along the way. Obviously you'd have to be accompanied, though. A young lady such as yourself, especially one so pleasing on the eye, shouldn't be out alone."

"You're far too kind," she told him.

"Bloodacre Farm isn't far out of my way," he continued. "If you were so willing, I could stop and call on you, and from your home I would be more than happy to accompany you on the journey to St. Margaret's. Your father would have to speak to me, so that he could be sure I'm to be trusted with you, but I believe that would be only a formality."

"You make a very kind offer," she told him, "but I have far too many jobs that must be done."

"Even on a Sunday?"

"My mother is confined to bed," she explained. "While she remains unwell, I have so many duties around the farm, and my father is suffering a little too. For now, I think I can only pray privately at home, and I must only hope that the Lord will show me mercy for that fact."

"Don't let your absence from the church last too long," the man replied darkly. "It would be easy to get drawn down the wrong path."

"I'm not quite sure what you mean."

"Perhaps I shall be more eloquent when next we meet," he said, before stepping closer and reaching out a hand for her to shake. "My name is Robert Potter and I must say, it has been a pleasure to speak with you."

"I feel the same," she said with a forced smile.

She hesitated, before realizing that his hand remained outstretched. Although she loathed the idea of touching another person's skin again, she knew that she would have to do so, at least if she wanted to avoid arousing any suspicions. She reached out and shook the man's hand, and she counted every excruciating second until finally she had no choice: pulling away, she forced a smile in the hope that she hadn't seemed too rude.

"I'm not sure," Robert said cautiously, "that I caught your name."

"Lydia," she replied nervously, and once again she worried that she must be on the verge of blushing.

"And do you have a surname, Lydia?"

"Smith."

"A common enough name," he said, before craning his neck a little as if he wanted to look behind her. "Are you holding something there, Lydia?"

Realizing that her attempts to hide the book had been futile, and aware that a denial would only make him ask more questions, she held the old volume out while trying to hide the stains.

"Just a book I... brought with me from home," she told him, terrified in case he wanted to examine the book more closely.

"You can read?"

"I can," she admitted. "I learned when I was younger. Father thought it might be useful so that I could help him when he's working."

"An admirable quality," Robert replied, "and a rare one around these parts, especially in a woman." He paused, seemingly lost in thought, before taking a step back. "Well, Lydia Smith," he continued, "I think I've seen and said more than enough. I enjoyed meeting you, and I hope I shall have the opportunity to speak with you again one day soon. And if you ever decide that you'd like to take me up on my offer, and have me accompany you on the walk to St. Margaret's, just come to the village and ask for me. I am well known around these parts."

"I shall," she replied politely, and then she felt a rush of relief as he turned and walked away.

Left standing alone, she watched as Robert disappeared around the corner. The man hadn't done or said anything particularly wrong, but he'd touched her twice and Lydia absolutely hated being touched by anyone. Still, she felt that she'd managed to seem fairly normal, and as she glanced back up at the front of Old Mother Marston's cottage she told herself that any danger had now passed. And then, as she looked at the bedroom window, she froze as she saw the face of an elderly woman glaring back down at her. For a few seconds, Lydia could only look back at the woman's old, sad eyes, and she felt bathed in a sense of doom.

"There you are!"

Turning, she saw that her father had made his way back along the street. She looked up at the window again, but now there was no sign of the old woman; the glass was dirty, however, and Lydia was already wondering whether in fact she'd merely been fooled by a trick of the light.

"So you didn't find anything?" Thomas asked.

"Nothing," she stammered, taking care to keep the book behind her back, hoping against hope that he hadn't spotted it already.

"Nor did I," he sighed, before stepping past her. "Come along, we might as well be going. This whole trip was a complete waste of time, although we'll take the long route home and hopefully we might find something along the way."

"Of course," Lydia said, glancing at the window once more and still seeing no sign of the woman, before hurrying after her father while keeping the book behind her back. "I'm sure you always know exactly where to look."

CHAPTER FIFTEEN

"SOME OF THESE PASSAGES make absolutely no sense to me," Lydia whispered under her breath a few hours later, as she sat on her bed in the farmhouse and peered at another page in the bloodstained book. "I can read the words, but I'm afraid I really don't understand their purpose."

She turned to the next page.

"There *is* a purpose, though," she added. "I don't know how, but I can just feel that this book isn't nonsense. There's a purpose that's almost... speaking to me, or trying to at least. I feel like such a fool for not understanding. Sometimes I wish I could be cleverer."

Hearing a purring sound, she turned to see that the black cat – which she still hadn't named – was cleaning himself on the other side of the bed.

As she watched the cat's efforts, Lydia couldn't help but marvel once again that the creature seemed to have become so much stronger and healthier in such a short space of time. Although he very clearly stayed away from her father, Lydia found that the cat always visited her when she was alone, and she'd come to find his presence strangely comforting. Reaching out, she stroked his side and heard his purring getting louder, and she realized in that moment that the cat was the only living thing whose touch she could bear.

"Sometimes I wish I could be a cat," she said softly. "I'd dearly like to just spend my days catching vermin, and otherwise enjoying the natural world. You don't have to endure any of the foolishness of human existence. We have a way of complicating everything, Mr. Cat, and I'm not sure that does us much good."

She began to scratch behind the cat's ear, and she smiled as he reacted by rolling onto his side and stretching his legs.

"You need a name, though," she added. "I could keep calling you Mr. Cat, but that doesn't seem very personal, does it?" She thought for a moment about the first time she'd seen the creature, when he'd been hiding behind a box in the storeroom, and suddenly she recalled the text written on the box's side. "Smythe Farm," she continued. "I suppose I could call you Smythe.

Would you like that name?"

As if in response, the cat rolled over and looked directly at her.

"Smythe it is, then," she said with a grin. "Do you think you can get used to it?"

Smythe blinked, and then he got to his feet and stepped closer. Settling against her side, he looked at the book, as if he too felt drawn to the various texts and images.

"Let this be your warning," Lydia read out loud, "that on this hallowed morning, never shall you fall or falter, so long as you withstand the water."

She paused.

"But what does it *mean*?" she asked with a heavy, frustrated sigh. "Is it just someone's attempt at rather bad poetry, or -"

Before she could finish, she heard the unmistakable sound of her father storming up the staircase. Filled with panic, she quickly hid the book beneath her tattered old bed-sheets, and Smythe jumped off the bed just as the door swung open and Thomas stepped into view.

"Were you talking to someone?" he snarled, glancing down briefly at Smythe before tuning to his daughter again. "You weren't talking to that cat, were you? I won't have any daughter of mine becoming simple-minded."

"Father," she replied, "I was just... singing."

"Singing?"

"Yes. To myself." She paused, hoping that he might believe the lie. "I'm sorry, though," she added. "I'll certainly make sure that I never do it again."

"I need help getting out of these clothes," he told her, clearly unconvinced. "You left some sacks close to the back door, and I hurt my back moving them. I've told you so many times that you mustn't leave things in the wrong places, and now I'm in pain again."

"I'm so sorry, Father," she replied, getting to her feet and wincing as she felt a tight pain in her own back. "I forgot to move them. I hope you can forgive me."

"You'll need to help me," he muttered, turning and heading through to one of the other bedrooms. "I'm exhausted but I'm not tired yet. You'll need to spend some time with me."

"Of course," she said darkly, clearly dreading the prospect as she limped after him. "It's okay, Smythe," she added, glancing back at the cat. "You can rest. I'll see you later."

Once Lydia had gone into the next bedroom and had shut the door, Smythe stood alone and watched the empty landing. Flicking his tail slightly, he listened to the sound of a bed creaking in one of the other rooms, and after a few seconds his eyes narrowed.

***

A low, cold wind blew across the desolate field beyond the edge of Almsford. Old dry grass ruffled gently, and a dirty river trickled narrowly through the landscape. After a moment, a pair of dirty boots jumped over the river – or what remained of the river, at least – before stopping on the half-dry mud.

Robert Potter took a moment to survey the landscape, watching the trees in the distance before finally his gaze settled upon a set of low buildings that stood silhouetted against the darkening grayish sky. He gaze narrowed slightly, and he knew now that he'd been right earlier; Bloodacre Farm was hiding some dark secret, and he felt a ripple of dread spreading through his bones.

"Is that it?" Esme Walker asked breathlessly as she finally caught up to him.

"There is something heathen in these lands," he murmured.

"What does that mean?"

"It means something wicked."

"That's where she lives," Esme continued, her voice filled with bitterness. "Her name's Lydia Smith. I've seen her in the village and I'm telling you, there's something about her that's no good."

"That much I have already seen for myself," he replied, keeping his eyes fixed on the distant farm.

"I'm sure you have," Esme said, looking up at the side of his face. "Everyone says you're a good man, Mr. Potter. You don't think I'd come out walking alone with just anyone from the village, do you? It's 'cause I trust you."

"You're right to do so," he told her.

"I want to be good," she added. "Not just good, I want to be perfect. In the eyes of the Lord, I mean. 'Cause that way, I think I might get rich."

"Is it truly only earthly delights that you seek?"

"No, I want the other things too," she countered. "I'm not shallow or weak, or anything like that." She paused again. "You said you'd walk me to St. Margaret's on Sunday, though. Are you still going to do that?"

"I believe it is the only way to save your wretched soul."

"And after that," she said cautiously, "once my... wretched soul has been saved, are you a man who's in need of a wife?"

He turned to her.

"I could be a good wife," she told him. "I'd do anything you asked of me, and I wouldn't ever complain. I've seen the way my own mother acts sometimes, and she needs taking down a peg or two. But I'd be obedient all the time and you wouldn't ever have to ask for anything. I'd anticipate your every need."

"You are a good young woman," he replied.

"And you're a good man," she said firmly, making an effort to maintain eye contact. "I think that's what I need, Mr. Potter. I'm after someone who can teach me how to be really good all the time. And if occasionally I get things wrong, if I stray from the righteous path or anything like that, would you..." Her voice trailed off for a few seconds. "Would you punish me?"

"I would have no choice."

"How would you do it?"

"How would I do what?"

"How would you punish me?" Her voice was tense with anticipation now; she was almost drooling. "Tell me all the details."

"There are many ways. It would depend very much upon the nature of your transgression."

"Oh." She thought for a moment. "Mr. Potter," she continued cautiously, "I've been good, I promise I have. I don't think I've made any transgressions, but I'm curious as to how *exactly* you'd deal with me if I had. If I was your wife, that is. I don't suppose, and I know that this is a big thing to ask, but is there any way you could demonstrate how you'd punish me? We could go somewhere, to a place where we won't get interrupted, maybe in the forest and... I'd very much like to experience just a little punishment. So that I know what to avoid."

"I think that can be arranged," he replied, before taking her by the hand and leading her along the side of the river, heading toward the darkness of the trees ahead. "You're a good girl, Esme Walker. You're not like some of the other foul creatures that live in these parts, but let me promise you one thing. They will soon receive their due."

"You mustn't hold back," she told him as they reached the edge of the forest and stepped between two of the trees, disappearing into the shadows. "I don't mind if you hurt me, Mr. Potter. In fact, I think I might quite like it."

CHAPTER SIXTEEN

A SOBBING SOUND DRIFTED through the house, emerging from the storeroom and slowly creeping its way across the hall and up the stairs. Sitting at the top of those stairs, Smythe stared back down at the empty hall and listened, tilting his head slightly as the sobbing continued.

A moment later, hearing a bed creaking in a nearby room as a heavy human weight shifted slightly, Smythe turned and looked across the landing. His eyes focused for a moment on one bedroom door, before finally he looked at the other, and now his tail flicked again.

***

Resting on his back, Thomas stared up at the ceiling

and wondered whether the pain would ever end. His daughter had left the room a few minutes earlier, but already Thomas could feel the discomfort returning to his back, and he knew that soon he'd be in agony once more. He considered praying, but he'd prayed before and the situation had only become worse. Deep down, he knew that life simply wasn't fair.

Suddenly hearing a clicking sound, he tried to turn his head so that he could look over at the door, only to find that his head wouldn't move at all. He blinked a couple of times, but to his surprise he realized that his eyes were the only part of his entire body that he was now capable of shifting. He could just about see that the bedroom door had slowly swung open, but there was no sign of anyone; he tried to open his mouth and call out, but even this proved impossible. Struggling to move, he felt as if every bone in his body had fused together and was now somehow stuck to the bed, leaving his helpless meat unable to offer any more than a strained defiance.

A moment later something bumped onto the bed. Trying not to panic, Thomas looked down and saw the twitching tail of Lydia's infernal black cat. After a couple of seconds, the cat calmly stepped fully into view, keeping his eyes fixed on Thomas.

"Help me," Thomas tried to say, but his jaw – like every other part of his body – refused to move even an inch.

The cat slowly made his way up the bed, before stepping onto the man's chest and finally stopping to look down at his face. Thomas stared back up at the animal, and in that instant he realized that he felt utterly powerless. The cat was purring slightly, and after a moment the creature sat down on his chest, still staring deep into his eyes.

"Lydia!" Thomas tried to call out, yet now his bones felt even more immobile, as if he was entirely paralyzed on his own bed.

And still the cat looked into his eyes, before slowly reaching out with one paw.

Thomas stared back at the paw, unable to shake a growing sense of dread, and he watched with horror as very slowly five razor-sharp claws emerged.

Instinctively trying to pull away, Thomas began to strain against his own bones, almost tearing the muscles away. He was just about able to look over at the window, but a fraction of a second later something moved in the corner of his vision; he looked at the cat again and saw the claws moving closer to his right eye, although the cat suddenly hesitated as if lost in thought.

And then, slowly, Smythe moved his paw down until the claws were gently touching the tip of the man's nose.

Terrified and confused in equal measure,

Thomas tried to focus on the claws, becoming almost cross-eyed in the process. After a moment one claw pressed against his nose, pushing into the skin, and Thomas realized that although he remained very much paralyzed, he could certainly still feel pain; indeed, he felt yet more pain as the cat twisted the paw and gouged away a chunk of his left nostril, then more and more pain as the creature began to dig into his nose, slowly tearing away chunks of flesh and leaving blood to dribble down the sides of his face. Unable to fight back, Thomas felt more blood running onto his lips as the cat's claws gouged deeper and deeper into the mound of his nose, finally striking bone.

For the next few minutes, working at an entirely unhurried pace, Smythe gradually tore off the rest of Thomas Smith's nose, finally leaving a bloodied stub exposing two ragged holes. Thomas felt an immense pain in the middle of his face, but he was unable to resist – unable to do anything except watch and blink – as the cat paused for a moment to admire the work he'd already completed.

"Help me!" Thomas cried out in his mind, hoping against hope that somehow his daughter might yet be able to hear him and could come to his rescue. "Lydia, this monstrous beast has lost its mind!"

He struggled as hard as he could manage, yet his body barely even twitched at all. Meanwhile

Smythe remained sitting on his chest, as if amused by the entire process, before eventually reaching down once again with his paw and starting to tear away more skin from where the nose had once been. As Thomas desperately tried to turn his head, Smythe methodically pulled away larger and larger chunks of bloodied flesh, ignoring the sprays of blood that flew up whenever Thomas let out a series of snorts, focusing instead on digging deeper and deeper. Soon a kind of pit or crater had been cleared in the center of the man's face, revealing the lines and curves of bone beneath.

Smythe hesitated again, as if assessing a new challenge. After a few seconds his tail flicked, and then he began to dig again, this time with more force.

Horrified, Thomas now felt pieces of bone cracking away from the area of skull beneath his destroyed nose. His struggles became even more frantic as he strained painfully against his own skeleton, but he remained powerless to resist as the cat began to crack open the front of his skull beneath the eyes, digging deeper while sending bloodied fragments of bone falling down onto either side of the bed. Finally Thomas heard the loudest crack of all, and he felt an immense sucking sensation as the cat lifted out a large plate of bone.

Now Thomas found that he could barely see anything at all as more blood dribbled into his eyes.

He had to blink furiously in an attempt to clear away any of the blood at all, and then he had to push through more pain as he looked down and tried to focus on the wretched evil monstrosity that even now was slowly dipping a paw into the hole it had created in his face.

Thomas felt the claws slicing into his head, going deeper still, and after a few more seconds he felt a strong tugging sensation that seemed to be coming from the center of his skull.

Slowly, with calm precision, Smythe began to pull his paw out from the hole. He had to tug a couple of times, but finally he lifted his paw up and stared at the clump of brain matter that he'd managed to dig out. After blinking a few times, he tossed the bloodied lump aside and resumed his excavations, digging just a little deeper this time and spending several more seconds at work before managing to lift out a slightly larger part of the man's brain.

Thomas, meanwhile, could barely even think at all, yet somehow beneath all the pain and fear a part of his mind was still screaming silently into the void. He knew he couldn't fight back now, and he knew that death was surely mere seconds away, yet he was filled with rage at the thought that Lydia hadn't rescued him. After all, she was the one who'd brought the disgusting evil little monster into the house, and now her pet was on the verge of murder. Thomas found himself actually longing for death, for an escape from the agonies of the world, yet he felt more blood gushing down the side of his face as the cat pushed its paw deeper yet, rooting around inside the mulchy mess as if reaching into an overflowing mass of meat. Blood was dribbling into the back of his mouth as Thomas felt the top of his throat collapsing, and now Smythe was ripping his claws carefully through the bowl of his brain, seemingly trying to select the part that he wanted to pull out next.

Finally Thomas felt the cat's claws reaching the back of his skull, digging into the stem, and then he watched in horror as Smythe pulled his paw out with thick, stringy brain matter caught on the sharp tips, extending the dribbling strands up and away from the bloodied face and purring all the while as -

"No!"

Gasping, Thomas blinked and sat bolt upright. Touching the front of his face, he was hugely relieved to find that his nose was still intact. He blinked again and looked around, and then he heard a creaking sound. Turning to the door, he saw a shape slipping out of sight, as if the cat *had* been in the room after all. Yet everything else, Thomas realized now with a sigh of relief, must have been nothing more than a nightmare. Even though his muscles ached terribly from his efforts to move while asleep, everything else had clearly been just a dream.

For the next few minutes, he merely sat on the bed, constantly touching his nose to make sure that it was indeed still intact.

CHAPTER SEVENTEEN

SMYTHE PURRED LOUDER THAN ever as he brushed against Lydia, pushing into her feet and then quickly turning to do the same from the other side.

"I know you're down there," she said, managing a smile as she continued to stir together the thick gray mixture in the bowl. "I'm just a little too busy at the moment to play. You must understand that."

Smythe moved around and pushed against her other leg with calm insistence, almost as if he was trying to tell her something.

"I must have food ready soon," Lydia continued. "Believe me, there'll be bedlam if I don't. I'm not like you, I can't just go into the storeroom and catch myself a nice dinner."

She looked at the rather disgusting slop she'd managed to prepare so far.

"Humans," she added uncertainly, "have... higher standards."

Hearing footsteps, she turned to see her father wandering into the room, although she immediately noticed that something seemed different. Stumbling slightly, as if he was barely able to stay on his feet, Thomas stopped just beyond the doorway and swayed; he reached out to steady himself, and as he looked around the room he seemed to be having trouble focusing on anything at all.

"Did you manage to sleep?" Lydia asked.

"Hmm?"

He turned to her, and for a few seconds Lydia couldn't shake the feeling that her own father seemed not to recognize her at all.

"Did you manage to sleep?" she asked again. "I thought you'd be up there for a while longer. Doesn't sleep help with the pain?"

"What would you... know about pain?" he asked groggily, before reaching up and touching his nose. "Stop peppering me with questions. I can barely think straight."

"Are you hungry?" she replied, puzzled by his insistence on feeling his own nose but supposing that there was no point asking too many more questions. "If you are, you'll find some bread on the side. I made it a few days ago but it should still be good."

She waited for him to reply, but already she was starting to wonder whether he'd even heard her words at all. Something about her father seemed, in that moment, to be terribly blank and vacant. Indeed, as she watched him looking around the room, she felt as if he almost didn't know where he was standing, as if he didn't recognize the kitchen.

"Why don't you sit down?" she said, stepping over to the table and moving a chair out. "Father, please, you're worrying me."

"I'm fine," he muttered, stumbling over and reaching out, grabbing her by the hand.

Flinching, Lydia pulled away.

"Why did you do that?" Thomas asked, before slumping down onto the chair. For a moment, he stared down at the bare table. "It's like... stepping through a hole in the air."

"What is?" she replied, more puzzled than ever.

"What?" He looked up at her. "I don't know. Girl, must you keep asking me so many questions? I didn't come down here just to have you make my head hurt like this! I came down to..." He looked around the room again. "I don't know why I came down. I just had to, that's all. And then -"

Spotting Smythe, he watched as the cat padded past.

"Eat this, Father," Lydia said, setting a plate of bread on the table. "I'll fetch you something to go with it." She made her way around the table, only to stop as her father once again grabbed her by the wrist. Hating the sensation of anyone touching her, she tried to pull away, and then she looked down at him. "Father," she continued through gritted teeth, "I shan't be long."

"That cat," Thomas sneered, keeping his eyes fixed on Smythe, "is the greatest evil this world has ever known."

"I rather fear," she replied, "that you aren't feeling well." She tried again to pull her wrist away, and to her surprise she was able to do so; she felt her father trying to keep hold of her, but his usual strength seemed to be missing. "Just stay here," she told him, "and I shall be back in a minute or two with something to go with the bread."

She waited for an answer, and then she wiped her hands on her apron as she headed out of the room.

"Smythe, keep an eye on him," she muttered as she walked past the cat. "I'm not sure what's going on, but it's almost as if he's drunk!"

***

"Yes, Mother!" she called up the stairs as she emerged from the storeroom with a plate of cheese.

"I heard you, and I shall be up in a minute or two! I'm just attending to Father first!"

"Of course you are!" Mary yelled back down at her. "He always gets *everything* first, and I'm always last!"

"This is decidedly not the case," Lydia muttered under her breath.

"What did you say?"

"Nothing," Lydia continued, struggling to stifle a sigh. She glanced at the door to the kitchen and watched as Smythe sauntered out; as he entered the hallway, the cat let his tail brush against the door's jamb. "Mother, I'll be up shortly. Father doesn't seem quite himself and I want to make sure that he eats, but then you'll be my absolute priority. I promise."

"A fat lot of good that'll do me," Mary grumbled as Lydia headed across the hallway, stopping briefly to stroke Smythe before continuing on her way to the kitchen. "I'll just sit up here and rot. That's all I'm good for these days, anyway."

"I found some cheese for you," Lydia said as she entered the kitchen. "Father, if -"

Stopping suddenly, she was horrified to see that her father was sitting chewing in front of the kitchen table, with blood dribbling down his chin. Several dead rats lay gathered on the plate in front of him, and Lydia watched aghast as Thomas picked up one of the rats and absent-mindedly bit into its flank, taking a moment to tear away the chest and then crunching hard on the bones as more blood ran down onto the table, splattering onto the plate and soaking the remaining rat corpses.

"Father, what are you doing?" Lydia gasped, scarcely able to believe such an awful sight.

"You told me to eat the bread," he replied calmly, smiling at her as he spoke with his mouth full, revealing the chewed meat and fur and shards of bone caked around his tongue. "Why are you looking at me like that? Sometimes I really can't quite fathom what's going on in your mind."

Before Lydia could stop him, he bit into the rat again, ripping open its belly and sending its organs slopping down onto the table. He quickly began to gather them up, pushing his fingertips into the stomach, bursting the sac as he lifted it up and slipped it into his mouth.

"It's not the usual bread you make," he said, spraying flecks of rat meat from his lips as he spoke. "Did you do something different to it this time?"

"Father, you must stop at once!" Lydia gasped, hurrying over and pulling the plate away even as her father reached for another rat. She set the plate on the side where he couldn't get to it, and then she tried to take the final remains from his hands. "Whatever are you doing? Do you have any idea how sick you're going to get?"

"*You're* the one who made the bread," he said innocently, struggling to hold onto the corpse. "Why are you being so funny about it all of a sudden?"

"Father, stop!" she hissed, horrified by the sight of rat fur caught between his teeth. "Have you lost your mind?"

Struggling to get the final rat from his hands, she tried to force his fingers away. When that didn't work, she had to step around to the other side, and finally she managed to pick most of the meat free even as Thomas slipped what he could into his mouth. She heard more bones splintering as he ate, and then as she pulled back she could only watch for a few seconds as he continued to chew. A moment later, once he'd swallowed, he got to his feet and began to make his way toward the plate, only for Lydia to snatch it away and hurry around to the other end of the room.

"Bring that back," Thomas said, with pieces of bone still in his mouth. A few of the shards were even embedded in his gums. "I'm hungry."

"You're insane!" she snapped back at him. "Do you realize that? Father, I think you need to see a doctor, this isn't normal behavior at all!"

"And what would you know about normal behavior?" he sneered. "You're just teasing me with that delicious food, offering it and then taking it away just when I've got the taste."

Reaching up, he pulled a few of the larger pieces of bone from his mouth; he stared at them, as if he wasn't sure where they'd come from, and then he tossed them aside. He reached into his mouth again and tried to remove a long splintered piece that had become embedded in his tongue.

"Stop playing foolish games," he continued, barely able to get the words out since his fingers were moving deeper into his own mouth all the time. "Don't make me punish you, Lydia. You won't like it if I have to punish you."

CHAPTER EIGHTEEN

AS SOON AS SHE was back up in her room, Lydia pushed the door shut and slid down onto the floor. She was still holding the plate of dead rats; she stared down at them for a few seconds, and then – suddenly seeing blood oozing from one of the corpses – she slid the plate away and sat shivering with fear on the floor.

"Lydia?" Mary shouted from one of the other rooms. "What are you doing? Why haven't you brought anything in for me?"

Lydia opened her mouth to reply, but at that moment she felt a retching sensation filling her belly. Before she had a chance to stop herself, she leaned forward and vomited, bringing up the meager meal of bread and butter that she'd eaten earlier; she quickly vomited again, then again, unable to stop thinking about the awful sight of her father eating all those dead rats.

And then, spotting movement nearby, she turned to see that somehow Smythe had made his way into the room with her. She watched him, and after a few seconds she began to feel a growing sense of suspicion.

"Did you have something to do with this?" she asked, her voice trembling with shock. "I don't even know how that would be possible, but..."

She hesitated, watching the cat as she realized that there was some strange knowing quality in his eyes. She told herself that she was wrong, that she had to be imagining things, yet somehow she felt sure that not only had the cat managed to get the rats onto her father's plate, but that he'd *known* exactly what he was doing in the process. A few seconds later Smythe began to step toward her, purring and twitching his tail, but Lydia began to feel an instant sense of revulsion.

"Leave me alone!" she yelled suddenly, kicking him in the side and sending him racing away behind the bed.

As soon as Smythe looked back around at her, Lydia realized that he'd done something that should be far beyond the capabilities of any cat.

"What are you?" she sneered, as Smythe slowly stepped out again. "Are you some kind of demon? Are you some form of devilish thing?"

As he moved closer, she tried to kick him again. This time she missed as Smythe skipped out of the way, and then she pulled back into the corner as she watched him edging past the bed. Finally he stopped and sat down, purring as he stared at her, and once more Lydia felt she could sense some kind of great intelligence emanating from his mind. She opened her mouth to tell him to leave her alone, but in that instant he raised one paw in a manner that seemed strangely familiar.

As she blinked, Lydia remembered the kitten she'd had as a child. Her mother had drowned the poor thing, but first Lydia had taught it a few tricks, including this gesture.

"It's not possible," she stammered. "That was years ago, and you died. Even if you hadn't died back then, you'd be far too old and..."

Her words faded to nothing, but already she was frantically thinking back to the book she'd read in the kitchen. One of the books from Old Mother Marston's cottage had contained what seemed to be spells, and Lydia was starting to realize that for some reason she was able to remember every single word that she'd read, as if the lines from the pages had burned themselves into her mind forever.

"Should you wish to never sleep," she whispered now, remembering the words from before, "I'll pray for you and never weep. Though you are dead, you shall yet rise, and open up your dusty eyes. You shall yet walk, as once before, and cast the dark into the morn. And..."

For a few seconds, she couldn't bring herself to say the next words.

"And live again," she added, as a cold shiver ran through her chest, "in shadow reborn. Draw life, from others torn."

Smythe stared back at her, almost as if he was relieved that she'd finally understood. She told herself that there was no way she could have inadvertently revived the cat, yet somehow in her addled mind that idea was starting to make sense.

"Why do I remember it?" she asked finally, keeping her voice down. "How is it that I remember every word from those books? I only read them once, they shouldn't still be in my head, yet... somehow they are."

She paused, before scrambling to her feet and hurrying across the room. Reaching into the wardrobe, she moved some clothes aside and pulled out the book she'd hidden earlier; this was the book she'd found under the floorboards at Old Mother Marston's home, and somehow it was this book in particular that seemed more potent than all the others. She made her way back to the bed and sat down, and then she began to frantically look through the pages until she came to one section that contained a set of particularly curious illustrations. For the first time, she felt as if she was starting to understand what she was seeing, as if the words and images were reaching out from the book and finding a way to sink into her thoughts.

"Three elements," she whispered, barely noticing as Smythe jumped up to sit next to her. "Air, water and fire. Everything is divided into those three elements, isn't it? That's the key to understanding everything else in this book."

She turned to another page and saw a set of spells. Whereas earlier these spells had seemed like gibberish, now they made total sense, as if the book had decided to teach her how to read its contents. Unable to tear her gaze away, Lydia read each page in turn, and she felt now as if some arcane new knowledge had begun to flood into her body and mind. Part of her was scared, terrified even, by the unnatural nature of what she was reading. She knew she was venturing into some darker world, to a place where she didn't quite belong, yet she also felt a growing sense of excitement and she knew she couldn't stop herself.

"It all makes sense," she said, unable to believe what was happening. "Why me? Why now? What am I supposed to do with all of this?"

Feeling Smythe bumping against her arm, she turned to him.

"Did *I* bring you back to life?" she asked, equally horrified and thrilled by that idea. "Were your bones rotting away in the grass for all those years, only for me to..."

Her voice trailed off.

"This is wrong," she added finally, before getting to her feet and throwing the book across the room. Suddenly horrified by the sense that she'd strayed into ungodly things, she backed against the wall as tears began to fill her eyes. "I've sinned," she stammered, telling herself that she'd only really read half the book yet fully aware that this was already far too much. "I shall surely burn in Hell for this. How can my soul ever be cleansed? I've done something awful and I deserve nothing more than..."

She hesitated, and already she could feel herself drawn back to the book. Filled with the sense that she could only be truly alive if she read to the end, she took a step forward before somehow finding the strength to stop herself. Torn between the urge to read the rest of the book and the desperate desire to be a good person, she remained frozen in place for a few seconds. Although she was so far just about managing to resist the book, she knew deep down that eventually she was going to break, in which case her only chance might be to burn the book entirely and hope that the ash could offer no further danger.

"I can do this," she said, stepping across the room and picking the book up in her trembling hands. Even now she wanted to rip it open, but she quickly resolved to do the right thing instead. "It must be gone forever."

She turned to go to the door, only to see Smythe standing in her way. Although she knew she could simply step over or around him, she felt that he was trying to block her progress.

"I don't have a choice," she told him. "I'm sorry, but I'm not a bad person. I mean, sometimes I'm wicked and greedy, but I always *try* to do the right thing." She sniffed back more tears. "I'd rather live the rest of my life in misery than dabble in some kind of... witchcraft."

Looking up at her, Smythe purred gently.

"I can't be a monster!" she sobbed, and now the tears were flowing freely down her face. "I shall burn this, and then I shall... I shall go to a convent, or if that's not possible I shall go to the church. I don't know if I can ever be forgiven for my sins, but I shall try. And if my soul is already blackened beyond all help, then that is my fault for allowing myself this moment of weakness."

Stepping around the cat, she opened the door and hurried out onto the landing. Reaching the top of the stairs, she stopped and turned to look into her mother's room. In that moment, she was so accustomed to her mother's constant nagging that at first she failed to note the silence.

"I shall be back up in a moment," she explained, wondering how she could ever explain her mistakes to her parents, "and -"

Before she could finish, she saw that her mother's bed was empty, with the top sheets pulled back to reveal the stained and blackened mattress beneath. Staring in horror, Lydia realized that she could see something moving in the depths of the mattress, and finally she realized that not only were there maggots wriggling in the fabric, but some had already dropped under the bed and were crawling across the boards.

And then, hearing an awful shrieking sound, she turned just as Mary lumbered out from the next bedroom. Before she had a chance to react, her mother slammed into her and sent her tumbling and screaming down the stairs.

CHAPTER NINETEEN

AS SOON AS SHE opened her eyes, Lydia realized that she must have been knocked out, at least for a few seconds. She blinked and looked around, and she found herself on the floor in the hallway. Sitting up, she felt more pain in her back, but as she turned to look around she saw no sign of her mother. A moment later, however, she heard frantic, whispered voices hissing conspiratorially in the kitchen.

Getting to her feet, she felt more and more sore, but she was relieved to find that she had no lasting injuries from her fall. She rubbed the back of her head as she tried to pull her thoughts together, and a moment later she saw Smythe making his way quickly down the stairs.

"Hey," she said, wincing slightly. "I don't quite know what happened but..."

Her voice trailed off as she once again noticed the voices in the kitchen. Although she didn't like to eavesdrop, she made her way quietly across the hallway and stopped to listen. Her mother was speaking rapidly and quietly, but as she leaned closer to the door Lydia was just about able to make out some of the words.

"I've had my suspicions about that girl for a while now," Mary was saying darkly, "and these books just prove it. There's something very wrong with her. Mark my words, we've raised a bad child and it's our duty to put things right. The Lord will judge us if we don't."

Silence fell for a moment, and Lydia felt Smythe briefly pressing against the side of her leg.

"You're no use," Mary continued with a sigh. "Marrying you, Thomas Smith, was the biggest mistake of my life. Do you see how that daughter of ours treats me? It's a wonder that I've been able to rise from my bed. I can't be sure, and I don't have any proof, but I wouldn't be at all surprised if that little whore has been poisoning me!"

Horrified by that accusation, Lydia opened her mouth to protest her innocence, but she held back as she realized that she wanted to hear more.

"And I know she has you under her spell," Mary added, her voice positively dripping with bitterness. "Don't think that I'm not aware of what goes on in this house, Thomas, because nothing gets past me. I know about it all, and I'm sick of everything. While I've been in my bed, this place has gone to the Devil, but it's all going to change from now on. Starting with that girl!"

Hearing footsteps, Lydia realized that her mother was on her way to the door. She stepped back, intending to hide, only for Mary to storm out into the corridor. Stopping, the older woman glared at Lydia with such venom that the younger girl instinctively took another step back, in the process bumping against the opposite wall.

"Don't think I haven't seen what you're up to," Mary sneered. "You have become a wicked and foul thing!"

"Mother," Lydia replied, "I only -"

"Your father is in a terrible state," Mary continued, "and I would have been left to rot away to nothing up there if I hadn't forced my poor body to rise Christ-like from that frame. You intended that to be my deathbed, but the Lord has given me the strength to revive and prove my devotion!"

"Mother," Lydia said, "I only wanted to -"

Before she could finish, she suddenly let out a heavy, painful hiccup. Shocked, she tried again to speak, but another hiccup came and then another; each gulp of air brought an excruciating pain to her chest, such that after a few more she had to support herself against the wall in an effort to remain on her feet.

"This is a sign from above," Mary snarled, as Lydia's hiccups became more frequent and much more painful. "This is the Lord's way of silencing your wicked lies!"

"Air!" Lydia stammered, barely able to get any words out at all as she clutched her belly. "So much air!"

Her knees began to give way, and as she once again steadied herself she realized that the world seemed to be swimming all around her. Feeling as if she might be about to collapse, she lowered herself down onto the floor while still hiccuping violently, and now she realized that her entire body seemed to be out of control. Tears were starting to stream from her eyes, and her mouth was filling with more saliva that she'd ever known before; after a few seconds, this overload of water started flowing from her lips.

"Look at her," Mary said, as Thomas limped out from the kitchen. "Look what our daughter has become, Thomas. I've heard of strange curses being rained down upon the unholy. They say there was a village of heathens nearby that was once visited by a plague of frogs, and now our own child is beset by this curious affliction."

In response, Thomas merely let out a faint groan.

"Help me!" Lydia gasped, looking up at her

parents and reaching out to them with one trembling hand. "I don't... I don't know what's -"

Suddenly another hiccup came, bursting through her chest with so much pain that she let out an involuntary cry. With more tears running from her eyes, she leaned forward onto her elbows, hoping desperately that this might provide some relief.

"I didn't need a sign," Mary said, glaring down at her, "but one has been delivered nonetheless. And now I am resolved that we must do whatever is necessary." She paused, before nudging the side of Lydia's face with her knee. "Girl, are you listening to me? Are you not even going to try to defend yourself, or have you finally found a modicum of shame?"

"Help me," Lydia said again, before whimpering as another hiccup burned through her body. Tears were falling faster from her eyes now, splattering against the wooden floorboards. "I don't understand. Why is this happening to me?"

"It's happening because no-one can hide forever from the judgment of the Lord," Mary explained, before nudging her face again. "You poor, pitiful, pathetic wretch, did you think yourself somehow special? Did you think you were better than the rest of us?"

"No," Lydia cried, "I merely -"

In that moment, Mary smacked her knee

into Lydia's face, knocking her to the side and sending her slumping down against the floor.

"Do not answer back!" she growled angrily. "How can you have the temerity for such things? Truly the Devil has taken hold of you and there is no hope. None at all. Fortunately, your father and I have a chance at least to show that *we* retain our faith."

"Please help me," Lydia sobbed, curling onto her side as she began to shiver violently on the floor, hiccuping every few seconds now. "I'm scared!"

"As you should be," Mary replied. "You are about to face your moment of judgment, and it's clear to me that you shall be found sorely wanting. You're going to burn in the pits of Hell, Lydia Smith, for all the cruelty you have visited upon me. I know what you are!"

Thomas managed another faint groan, but his eyes seemed curiously unfocused, as if he was barely aware of his surroundings. A dribble of clear liquid was running from one of his nostrils.

"I've never done anything wrong!" Lydia cried.

"Then how do you explain those books you've been reading?" Mary asked. "Did you think your father and I wouldn't find them? You've been reading those scraps that came from the village, and they've turned your already addled mind into a festering nest of sin and villainy."

Spotting movement at the end of the corridor, Lydia saw Smythe watching from a distance. She reached out toward him, hoping that somehow he could help, but he simply kept his eyes trained on her as his tail flicked.

"Please," Lydia gasped, "I don't..."

In that moment, as another hiccup burst through her body, she thought back to the book she'd hidden in her room. Looking around, she tried to spot the book, but when she glanced up at her mother she received her answer; Mary was holding that particular book, and Lydia realized that she must have dropped it when she fell down the stairs.

"Thomas," Mary said calmly, "drag her outside. We have to do what is right."

"Wait," Lydia whispered as her father stepped around behind her and hauled her up, holding her by the shoulders. "I think... I remember now..."

"Take her out of the house," Mary continued, glaring into her daughter's eyes. "I know exactly how she must meet her end."

"Air," Lydia stammered, before hiccuping again.

"I'm going to enjoy this," Mary added, narrowing her gaze a little. "I'm going to take great pleasure from every last drop of blood that we spill from her veins."

"Water," Lydia added, as more and more tears flowed from her eyes, dribbling freely onto the floor below.

"What are you waiting for?" Mary asked. "Thomas, this is no time for delay. We've done enough of that already. Take her outside while I find a suitable knife."

"And...."

Lydia's voice trailed off for a few seconds, before her father turned her around, forcing her to look into his face. At that moment, she saw not only the pained blankness in his eyes but also the bloodied grayish liquid that was now flowing from both his nostrils and soaking the stubble of his unshaven beard.

"And fire," Lydia said softly, feeling a rising sense of anger starting to move up through her body. "Air, water and fire!"

With that, she pulled back and screamed as loud as she could manage, and to her horror a vast wall of flames burst through the air all around. The last thing she saw was the sight of her father's face burning away before her very eyes, and the last thing she heard was her mother's agonized scream.

CHAPTER TWENTY

THE LIGHT OF DAY was starting to fade now, turning the sky a deepening shade of blue beyond the silhouetted trees as Lydia stumbled across the rough mud a short distance from the house. She took a few more steps, dazed and unable to quite comprehend what had just happened, and then she turned and looked over her shoulder.

The farmhouse was nothing more now than a burned, smoldering ruin. The ceiling had collapsed, crushing the lower parts of the building, and the entire place was almost unrecognizable. The inferno had lasted for only a couple of minutes, or at least that was how it had seemed, but somehow even the brick walls had been almost completely destroyed. She'd lost track of the awful sounds – of the screams from her parents as well as the roar of the flames – and she didn't even know how she'd made it out of the fire. Somehow she'd simply begun to walk, and now she felt utterly cold and strangely calm as she continued to stare at the wreckage of Bloodacre Farm.

Hearing a rustling sound, she turned to see Smythe picking his way around puddles of muddy water on the ground, slowly making his way closer.

"I didn't mean to do it," Lydia whispered, barely strong enough to speak at all. "I never -"

Stopping suddenly, she realized that her crippling hiccups were gone. She reached up and touched her cheek; her eyes were sore and felt slightly swollen from all the crying, but after a few more seconds she looked down at the front of her dress and noticed one more strange matter.

She was unburned. Her flesh and clothes hadn't been touched by the flames at all. Even her hair had survived without so much as a singed end.

"You're okay," she continued, looking down as Smythe brushed against the side of her leg. "You made it out too. Smythe, for a few seconds there I felt as if I was completely out of control. My body... it was as if all of that came rushing out unbidden and I could barely hang on as..."

Again, her voice trailed off. She looked at the smoking ruins of the farmhouse once more, and she briefly considered going back to try to rescue her parents. She knew, however, that there was no point; she'd heard her mother's cries, and she'd seen the heat and fire burn her father's face away, and she'd watched as he'd toppled backward with a shocked expression and had been engulfed by the flames. She flinched slightly as she remembered that moment, but a few seconds later she felt Smythe once again brushing against her leg, almost as if he was trying to catch her attention for some terribly important reason.

"I feel different," Lydia whispered, before holding her hands up and peering more closely at her uncharred skin. "I feel as if there's something in me now that wasn't there before. It's almost a kind of..."

She paused, searching for the right description before realizing that there was only one word that made any sense at all.

"Power."

***

Once she reached the outskirts of the village, Lydia knew that she really had nowhere to go. She wandered along the dirty, muddy street that led past the first houses, and she even began to wonder why she'd walked to Almsford at all. There was nothing in the village for her, she had no family or friends there, and as she stopped and looked at the dark little houses she began to fear that she might be asked difficult questions.

She hesitated for a few more seconds, with Smythe still by her side, and then she turned around so that she could walk back the way she'd just come.

"Are you alright?"

Stopping, she realized that she recognized the voice. She turned to her left and saw a figure moving in the darkness of a nearby garden. After a few seconds the figure stepped forward, and Lydia realized that this was one of the girls she'd met in the village before, although she wasn't quite sure of her name. Then again, Lydia had never much mixed with the people of the village at all; her family had always been seen as poor outsiders, scrabbling to survive on the farm.

"I saw flames in the distance," the girl continued, making her way past the gate and finally stopping in front of Lydia. "A few of us did, actually. They seemed to be coming from somewhere out near Bloodacre Farm."

"There was an... accident," Lydia said, not really sure how else to explain what had happened.

"You look dreadful," the girl said, stepping closer and reaching out to put a hand on the side of Lydia's arm. "You simply can't be allowed to wander around like this. Are you going anywhere in particular?"

"No," Lydia replied, barely able to even

think about the question. "Yes. I mean... no. I mean, I don't think so."

"Then you must come with me," the girl said, taking hold of her hand and forcing Lydia to follow her along the dark street. "My father and some other men just went out toward Bloodacre Farm, I believe, to see whether there's any trouble. I expect they'll be back soon. Tell me, do you know whether everyone got out safely?"

"They didn't," Lydia explained. "My parents... I think they died."

"How awful. But you escaped?"

"I'm not really sure how," Lydia continued, sounding almost as if she was in a trance. Down at her feet, Smythe was keeping pace. "It all happened so very quickly. One minute there was no fire at all, and then all of a sudden the whole place was ablaze."

"That sounds terribly exciting. No, I'm sorry, that's not quite the right word. It sounds awful. That's what I meant to say. What exactly caused the fire in the first place?"

"I'm not entirely sure that I know."

"I bet it was the chimney," the girl said, "or the hearth. My father says that those things can cause awful trouble if they're not tended to properly, and a house can burn down in a matter of minutes. Oh, I'm so sorry that something like this has happened to you, you seem like such a nice girl."

"I'm not so sure about that," Lydia whispered darkly.

"My mother will see that you're alright," the girl continued. "She's very good at that sort of thing. I'm so lucky to have her. Oh, but I don't mean to brag or anything like that. I'm afraid I have a terrible habit of putting my foot in everything, and I say things that I really shouldn't. Mother's always reprimanding me and I try to do better, but I get it wrong time and again. And now I'm waffling, which is another of my failings. I do hope you can forgive me."

"There's nothing to forgive," Lydia replied. "Where are you taking me? I feel as if I shouldn't be causing you any trouble."

"It's no trouble at all," the girl said firmly, tightening her grip on Lydia's hand. "You're so cold. Isn't that strange? Your entire family just died in a horrible fire, yet you're as cold as ice."

"I suppose it's complicated."

Down at her feet, Smythe was still keeping up, while occasionally bumping against the side of her foot.

"Here we are," the girl said, leading Lydia off the street and into a nearby garden, then heading straight to the front door of a small cottage. "Home sweet home. Mother will be more than happy to help you out, and we even have a spare bedroom that you can sleep in. It's not as if you can go home, is it?"

"I don't want to be a burden."

"Don't be so silly," the girl continued, opening the door and then almost shoving Lydia inside. "Mother!" she called out. "We have a visitor! It's Lydia Smith from Bloodacre Farm, there's been the most terrible accident and now she's an orphan!"

"What's that?" an older woman asked, drying her hands on a cloth as she hurried through from the back of the cottage. "You poor thing, you look awful." She stopped and looked into Lydia's eyes. "We're going to have to get you warmed up, aren't we? Come along, you can tell me what happened."

Without waiting for an answer, she began to lead an almost zombie-like Lydia up the stairs.

"Do be sure to look after her," the girl called out as she watched them reaching the landing. "I'm Esme, by the way. Did you hear that, Lydia? My name's Esme and I just want to be your friend!"

Hearing a meowing sound, she turned to see that Smythe was entering the hallway.

"Get out of here!" she hissed, rushing over and kicking the cat back out onto the step. Smythe instantly let out an angry hiss, but Esme kicked him again before slamming the door shut with such force that it rattled in its frame. "We don't want vermin in our house, thank you very much!"

She peered out through the window, and to her relief she saw Smythe slinking away along the garden path. She watched until the cat was entirely out of sight, and then she turned and looked at the staircase as she heard her mother fussing over Lydia in one of the rooms above.

"It would seem that we have a new friend," Esme said softly, licking her lips as she began to smile, "and a house guest to boot. Mr. Potter's going to be *so* happy with me."

CHAPTER TWENTY-ONE

"THERE WAS NOTHING THERE that could possibly be salvaged," Arthur Walker said a few hours later, as he stood in the cottage's candlelit front room. "We searched through the ruins, but the fire must have been very strong. I've honestly never seen such devastation."

"Did you hear that?" Esme asked, turning to Lydia as the two girls sat together on one of the benches. "You can't possibly go back. You'll *have* to stay with us now."

"Someone's gone to speak to the priest now," Arthur continued, watching Lydia's strangely expressionless face closely. "You'll probably have to talk to him tomorrow. Just to... make a few arrangements." He waited for an answer. "Did you hear what I just said?"

"Yes, I'm sorry," Lydia replied, looking up at him again. "You've been so kind already, and I really don't want to cause you any more trouble. I think I should be going now."

"Don't be foolish!" Esme said quickly, putting an arm around her to keep her down. "You've got nowhere to go!"

"I -"

"Your parents are dead," Esme added, "and your home has burned to a crisp. You're an orphan. You have no family whatsoever. What are you thinking to do? Sleep on the ash?"

"Where's Smythe?" Lydia asked, looking around the room. "Has anyone seen my cat?"

"No idea," Esme told her. "He's probably just run off, though. Cats are like that. They have absolutely no loyalty, you know."

Lydia turned to her, and for the first time in hours she looked genuinely troubled.

"I'm sure he'll find a new home," Esme continued, unable to stifle a grin, "just as you've found one." She looked across the room just as her mother made her way through. "That's right, Mother, isn't it?" she added. "Can Lydia stay with us for now? I'll do all the extra work that's necessary while she rests, you'll barely even know that she's here. You wouldn't send her away when she's all by herself and has nobody else, would you? Would you be so cruel to someone who's sitting here with absolutely nothing and no-one left in the whole big wide world?"

"Of course not," Erica replied, setting a a jug of water on the table next to Lydia. "You poor thing," she said softly. "You must understand that we're here to look after you. We've always considered ourselves to be good, Christian people, and it's no trouble at all to take in someone who has clearly suffered so much. I shall pray for you before I go to sleep tonight, Lydia. I'm sure the whole village will pray for you."

"They shouldn't," Lydia whispered.

"Why not?" Esme asked.

"Forget it," Lydia said, getting to her feet. "I have no doubt that you're good Christian people, but I really don't think I should be here. You've already been so kind, but I need to find my cat and then I'll be out of your hair."

"Absolute nonsense," Erica said. "You're staying with us for now, and that's the last word." She turned to her husband. "Will you let the priest know that Lydia's here whenever he needs to talk to her?"

"If that's how things are going to be," Arthur said, casting a skeptical glance at Lydia before turning and heading out of the room. "It's not like I get any input round these parts. I just go to work every day and exhaust myself, and everyone else makes the decisions in my house."

"You'll be just fine here," Esme told Lydia, before pulling her closer and hugging her tight. "You've got us now!"

***

"Is there nothing else you need?" Esme asked a while later, as she stepped into the bedroom and saw that Lydia was still sitting on the edge of the bed and looking somewhat lost. "Oh, you seem so sad. Why don't I sleep in here with you tonight?"

"No, please," Lydia replied, before pausing for a moment. "You and your family have been so kind already. I don't want to put you out any further."

"You're not putting anyone out," Esme said, making her way over and looking down into Lydia's eyes. "Why must you persist in acting as if you're a burden when you're nothing of the sort? You know, I think you and I might even end up being really good friends!"

"Has anyone said anything about the fire?" Lydia asked.

"Just that it was awful and huge. And quick."

"But has anyone talked about how it might have started?"

"Not that I'm aware of," Esme said, before kneeling in front of Lydia. "Why? How *did* it start?

I'm not sure if you ever quite explained that part."

"I'm not sure that I can."

"Why not?"

"Because it seemed to come from..."

Lydia paused for a few seconds, before turning and looking at the open doorway. As a nearby candle flickered, she waited to make sure that Esme's parents weren't nearby, and then she let out a sigh; turning to Esme again, she told herself that she shouldn't breathe a word to anyone about what had happened, yet she also felt desperate to get the truth out. She hesitated, still terrified about how her new friend might react, but already she knew she wasn't going to be strong enough to keep her mouth shut.

"I think it was... my fault," she admitted finally.

"*Your* fault?" Esme replied, furrowing her brow. "How?"

"I don't want anyone to hate me."

"How could anyone hate you?" Esme asked. "Was there some kind of accident?"

"You mustn't tell anyone."

"I won't, I promise."

"It wasn't on purpose."

"I never dreamed that it could have been."

"My mother could be so angry at times," Lydia explained cautiously. "Especially recently, while she's been ill. And my father... I suppose the less said about him the better. But today Mother really exploded with rage after she found... well, she got some ideas into her head about things that I might have been doing. She wasn't wrong, but she didn't give me a chance to explain."

"Did you argue?"

Lydia nodded.

"That's alright," Esme pointed out. "Everyone argues occasionally."

"Not like this," Lydia told her darkly. "Not with so much anger. And I doubt very much that anyone else has ever..." Her voice trailed off again; she felt so foolish even thinking these things, let alone saying them out loud. "The fire," she added finally, "didn't come from the hearth, or from the chimney, or anything like that. The fire came from..."

Her voice trailed off again.

"I mean..."

"It's alright," Esme said softly. "You can tell me anything."

For a few seconds Lydia imagined blurting out every last part of the story. At the same time, she was terrified that she might end up attracting the wrong sort of attention, so she decided – at least for now – to try to avoid the worst of the details.

"I'm really not sure exactly what happened," she explained finally, while promising herself that at least on some level she wasn't lying. Not exactly. "I don't think I even want to find out. I think some things might be better left as mysteries. Why are you asking me all these questions?"

"I was just wondering, that's all," Esme replied, as the candle's reflected light danced in her eyes. After a moment she got to her feet and stepped back. "But that's something we should think about in the morning, when you're more rested. Right now I think you need a good night's sleep, and we'll talk more tomorrow." She turned and headed to the door, taking a moment to blow out the candle before looking back at Lydia again. "I think we're going to be really good friends," she added. "I just can't wait for all the fun we're going to have together!"

***

Outside in the dark street, Smythe sat on the grass and watched as the light was snuffed out in the cottage's window. He waited for a few more seconds, before turning and walking away, heading all alone along the winding street that led out of the village.

CHAPTER TWENTY-TWO

"SO DO YOU EVEN know Almsford very well?" Esme asked the following morning, as she and Lydia made their way along a street near the village green. "I've seen you around once or twice, but not very many times."

"I have a vague idea of the place," Lydia admitted, as she spotted yet another woman glaring at her from a nearby cottage. "I can't say that I have too much experience, though."

"It must have been very lonely, living out there at Bloodacre Farm," Esme said, leading her across the street. "I suppose you were very busy most of the time, but still, it must be hard not to have any friends." Reaching the stone steps leading up into the cemetery, she swung her arms a little as she walked. "Don't worry, though," she added, "because everything always works out for the best. That's why it must have been fate that you and I would meet like this."

Lydia stopped at the bottom of the steps and looked up, as Esme stopped just past the gate and turned to look back down at her.

"Where are we going?" Lydia asked cautiously.

"Is something wrong?"

"I just... where exactly are you taking me?"

"Why are you asking me that?" Esme continued. "Isn't it obvious?" She paused for a moment, watching Lydia carefully. "You don't mind coming into the churchyard, do you? There's not some... reason why you'd be against that, is there? It's just a load of old stones, with bodies buried deep beneath in... I suppose the ground is hallowed, whatever that means. It's more spiritual and good somehow. Christian and decent. The kind of place where evil can't exist. Does that bother you?"

"No, of course not," Lydia replied, forcing herself to make her way up, even though she felt distinctly uneasy. A cold wind blew against her, almost as if the elements themselves were trying to warn her that she was making a mistake.

"I always love coming to the cemetery," Esme said merrily, as she turned and began to make her way between the tilted gravestones. Reaching out, she ran her fingertips against their tops, making a show of feeling the rough stone edges and the gathered collections of thick yellowing moss. "It's a very spiritual place. A very *religious* place. I suppose you're going to think that I'm awfully strange, but I feel safer here than anywhere else. It's almost as if, in a cemetery, I know that the Lord is protecting me and that nothing bad or unholy or evil can enter."

She turned to look again at Lydia, who'd stopped at the top of the steps and hadn't quite set foot in the cemetery yet.

"Are you coming in?" Esme asked sweetly.

Lydia swallowed hard, before stepping forward. As soon as her right foot pressed against the grass, she braced for a bolt of lightning to flash down and burn her to a crisp; when that failed to occur, she felt a sense of relief but also a growing flicker of foreboding. At least a bolt of lightning would have been quick, and as she glanced around she still felt sure that the Lord wouldn't want someone like her being in such a holy place. After all, she wasn't quite sure of her own powers and she wasn't sure what she'd become, but she knew one thing.

Her powers weren't natural.

"You silly goose," Esme laughed.

Lydia turned to her.

"You look absolutely scared stiff," the other girl continued, before hurrying over and taking her by the hand. "There's no reason for that, you know. I'm your friend and I'd never let anything bad happen to you. Now, why don't we find a nice shady patch and sit down? Then we can natter away without anyone bothering us. Doesn't that sound like a great idea?"

***

"I probably shouldn't tell you this," Esme said a short while later, as they sat together in the shade of an old oak tree at the far end of the cemetery, "but everyone's talking about you."

"They are?" Lydia replied.

"Well, about your family," Esme continued, twiddling a plucked daisy between her fingers. "About the farm. Well, about all of it. What went on, I mean." She watched the daisy for a moment longer before squeezing the head between her fingertips, crushing it completely. "People in Almsford love to gossip, and they're all wondering exactly what caused the fire."

"I bet they are," Lydia muttered under her breath.

"They're also wondering about the fact that you -"

Suddenly Esme fell silent for a few seconds.

"Well," she added softly, "I suppose I shouldn't say that part."

"What part?"

Lydia waited for an answer.

"Tell me," she said firmly.

"They're just wondering how you came out of it all so unharmed," Esme continued, as she plucked another daisy and began to remove the petals one by one. "There's not a scratch on you, is there? Now, I told them all that you were just lucky, that sometimes these things happen. Still, they keep on gossiping. Even Father has asked me a few times. I know that when you were washing the other day, he watched you through the crack in the door."

"He did?" Lydia replied, horrified by that suggestion.

"Just to make sure you didn't have any marks or burns on your body," Esme explained. "It was a perfectly natural thing for him to do. I suppose he hoped to spot a few things that might make him less worried."

"I didn't know that people found me so fascinating," Lydia said through gritted teeth. "I shouldn't have come here. I need to think about where I'm going to go next."

"Go?"

"I can't stay with your family forever."

"Why not?"

"I just can't," Lydia replied, before looking around the cemetery. "Have you seen my cat? I thought he might come back this morning, but there's no sign of him."

"Lydia -"

"Smythe?" she called out, hoping against hope that he might appear soon. "Smythe, where are you? Can you hear me?"

"I'm sure he's long gone," Esme told her.

"I thought he liked me," Lydia continued, before sighing as she turned to Esme again. "Then again, I suppose you might have been right. Cats don't have much loyalty, do they?"

"Not like us humans," Esme countered, still focusing on the daisy as she pulled it apart piece by piece, dissecting it down to the tiniest piece. "Obviously you have to be careful who you trust. We're not all equal, are we? Some of us are deceitful liars, and some of us..."

She paused, before finally looking over at Lydia again and meeting her gaze.

"You know you can trust *me*, don't you?" she added. "I'd never betray you, and I'd never pass along anything you told me in confidence. If there's something about, say, the fire and how it started, or about how you survived without a scratch... you can tell me. Honestly. I'm your friend."

"I know," Lydia replied. "You keep reminding me."

"I just think it must be so hard to carry a burden," Esme suggested. "I'd hate for you to feel weighed down by something like that. You know,

Lydia, you can tell me anything. Anything at all."

Lydia opened her mouth to insist that there was nothing she'd been holding back, but deep down she knew that she was hiding a secret. The idea of talking to someone – anyone at all – about what had happened felt so compelling, even if she knew deep down that most people would be horrified by the truth. She thought back to the sight of her father being consumed by the flames, and to the cries of her mother. What person in their right mind wouldn't recoil in terror and run away upon hearing of such things? Looking down at her own hands for a moment, she felt as if she must have become possessed by some kind of devilish power, and she realized that she rued the day when she'd ever picked up the first of those old books.

"Do you have any secrets?" Esme asked, her voice positively dripping with apprehension and excitement. "Do you, Lydia? It's just that I thought last night, for a moment, you seemed to be on the verge of telling me something."

Looking at her, Lydia felt for a moment as if her own chest might explode. At the same time, Esme Walker was the closest she'd ever come to making a friend, and she hated the idea of losing her already.

"No," she lied finally, hating herself even more in that moment. "There's nothing."

"Are you sure?"

Lydia nodded.

"Well," Esme replied cautiously, "I'm really not sure that I believe you, but perhaps you'll tell me when the time feels right. A burden shared is a burden halved, after all."

"There's really nothing," Lydia said, even though she knew she was a terrible liar and she could see the disbelief in her new friend's eyes. "I swear. There's nothing interesting or unusual about me at all."

CHAPTER TWENTY-THREE

SITTING CROSS-LEGGED ON THE floor in the Walkers' spare room, Lydia stared at the torn and ruined daisy on the wooden floorboards. Having watched Esme dissect daisy after daisy in the cemetery earlier, Lydia had secretly collected one for herself. All through dinner she'd been contemplating an idea, and now she was alone.

The time had come.

Although she wasn't sure how, she still found herself able to remember every single page from the old books. All the words and images had burned themselves into her mind, and while she felt a slight ache in her head whenever she thought about them, she couldn't help going over and over the strange lines; in some manner, she knew that she understood those books, even if she couldn't shake a sense of fear. And as she looked down at the shredded daisy, she also knew exactly which part of the oldest book could be used to bring it back to life.

"You who grew in fields afar," she whispered now, "and called aloud your beauty mute."

Hearing a floorboard creaking out on the landing, she turned to look at the door. She'd been careful to shut the door properly, but she still waited a few seconds to make sure that she wasn't being watched through some hidden crack. Finally she looked down at the daisy again.

"Though now you rest here, dry and dead," she added, remembering the rest of the words from the book, "return to life, and grow your root."

She swallowed hard, and after just a brief moment she realized that the daisy was starting to twitch slightly. The crushed part of the stem began to move, as if becoming moist again, and one by one the broken little white petals reattached themselves to the reforming yellow head. At the bottom of the stem, meanwhile, tiny roots were starting to emerge as if in search of soil, and Lydia realized with a growing sense of awe and wonder that she'd actually succeeded in bringing such a precious and fragile thing back to life.

Finally she picked the daisy up and held it aloft, and she saw that it appeared entirely healthy now, albeit in rather dire need of replanting.

"I did it," she said softly, keeping her voice low. "It actually works. It's even -"

Suddenly she heard another creaking sound. She looked over her shoulder, yet still she saw no sign of anyone. At the same time, she couldn't shake the sense that she was being watched, and she thought back to Esme's rather creepy claim earlier about Arthur. If he'd been watching her while she bathed, wasn't there a chance that he had a view into the spare bedroom as well? Holding her breath, she continued to look all around, before returning her attention to the daisy and marveling at the sight of its roots, which even appeared to have grown a little longer in the previous few seconds.

"You're alive again," she continued. "Just like... just like Smythe was alive again, and... and that time, I didn't even do it on purpose. You're alive and -"

Hearing yet another creaking sound, she glanced briefly across the room. At first she assumed that the little cottage was merely settling as the temperature dropped, but after a moment – to her horror – she spotted a single eye staring back at her through a hole in the wall.

***

"I'm not angry!" Esme hissed, as she stood in the

garden and watched Lydia replanting the daisy by moonlight. "I understand why you lied to me. I just want to help you, that's all."

"I don't need help with anything," Lydia replied, taking care to pack some soil around the daisy's regrown roots, unable to look up and make eye contact. "Don't worry, you won't have to put up with me for much longer. I'm going to leave tonight."

"And go where?"

"That's none of your concern."

"Of course it's my concern," Esme said, sounding exasperated as she stepped around Lydia and knelt opposite. Bathed in moonlight, she watched for a moment as she continued to work. "I know what I saw up there. You -"

"You didn't see anything!" Lydia hissed angrily, finally meeting her gaze.

A moment later, spotting movement nearby, both girls turned to see that Erica Walker was at the upstairs window. For a moment Esme's mother looked down at them, before drawing the curtains.

"I haven't told them anything," Esme whispered. "I promise."

"There's nothing to tell," Lydia replied, sniffing back tears of frustration and shame.

"You brought that daisy back to life," Esme continued. "You can't hide it from me, not now. I know you can do special things, Lydia, and I think it's wonderful."

"It's sinful!" Lydia snapped.

"No, it's beautiful."

"It's against nature."

"Why?" Reaching out, Esme took hold of Lydia's hands, squeezing them tight. "Have you stopped to consider the possibility that you're *meant* to be able to do this? Oh, I know men like Robert Potter like to rant against such things, but that's just because they don't understand. Or they're scared. The world is full of silly scared little men who just want to ruin everything for other people, but we can't let them. Lydia, I've heard of people like you before. I think Old Mother Marston in the village had these powers too, and she was forced to hide away. You have a chance to do something different."

"Please," Lydia replied, as tears ran down her face, "stop talking about it."

"No, I won't," Esme said, "because it's a rare and precious thing."

She paused, before reaching down and pulling the daisy out, then twisting its head off and throwing the remains down onto the grass.

"Do it again," she said breathlessly. "Go on, Lydia, let me see you do it close up!"

Lydia shook her head.

"Why not?"

"Because it's wrong and immoral."

"I just told you, it's -"

"I killed my parents with it!" Lydia snarled, before she had a chance to stop herself. Realizing her mistake, she stared at Esme and waited for her reaction.

After a few more seconds, Esme started to laugh.

"It's not funny," Lydia told her.

"Oh, but it is," Esme replied, barely able to get the words out as her laughter continued. "You can be so serious sometimes, Lydia. It's almost too much to listen to!"

"I burned the farm down," Lydia explained, "and I burned my parents along with it. I didn't mean to, but it's as if this power just came bursting out of me. I read some books that Old Mother Marston had left behind, and now I can't forget what was in them. I brought Smythe back to life without meaning to, and then I caused the fire that destroyed the farm and killed my parents, and that makes me a wicked thing."

"No," Esme said firmly, grabbing her hands again and squeezing tighter than before. "It makes you an amazing, wonderful thing!"

"I don't want these powers," Lydia told her. "I hate them."

"Then give them to me," Esme replied. "Or share them, at least. Teach me how to do what you're doing."

"I can't."

"Of course you can," Esme continued excitedly. "Anything can be taught, you just have to be clever about it. Make the daisy come to life again, and talk me through it. Better still, tell me the magic words I need to use."

"It's not as simple as that," Lydia replied. "At least... I don't think so."

"Do you know what I think?" Esme asked, her eyes wide with anticipation now. "I think this is something that only women can do. I think it's a gift, given to us to make up for the way we're treated by men. It's probably why men hate us so much!"

"I'm not sure that -"

"And I think it's any woman's duty to share it with other women," Esme added. "It's our way to fight back, our way to make ourselves strong when they want to make us weak. Lydia, you *have* to teach me, and then I'll teach others. Only the ones who deserve to be taught, of course. Only the ones we can trust. But we'll spread this knowledge far and wide, Lydia, and then who knows? Perhaps one day we shall all rise up like an army and cast off our oppressors, and then we'll finally show them all who's really got the power."

Staring back at her, Lydia could barely believe the words that had just come from her friend's mouth.

"No," she said finally, shaking her head. "Absolutely not. Not in a million years."

"Lydia -"

"No!" Lydia snapped, pulling back and stumbling to her feet. "You really don't understand, do you? You have no idea what this power could do to the world. It's not something to be celebrated or shared! It's something to be hidden away! It's shameful and wrong and it must never be revealed to anyone!" She paused, but already she was starting to realize that she should have left earlier. "I'm sorry you had to see any of this, Esme," she added. "It wasn't fair of me to give you this burden."

"At least think about it," Esme replied. "Will you promise me that? Sleep on it, and in the morning see if you feel any better. You might find that in the cold light of day, you have more sensible thoughts and you're willing to consider my offer."

"I need to be alone," Lydia said, turning and hurrying back into the cottage. "I need to think."

"Don't take too long," Esme muttered under her breath, standing in the moonlight and watching as Lydia disappeared up the stairs. "My offer won't stand forever."

CHAPTER TWENTY-FOUR

SOMEWHERE OFF IN THE distance, an owl hooted.

Standing in the pitch-black spare bedroom, Lydia knew that the time had finally come. She'd shut the door over an hour earlier, and then she'd waited until she'd heard Esme retiring to one of the other bedrooms; then she'd waited some more, determined to hold off until she could be absolutely certain that the Walkers were all asleep. Although she hated the idea of letting them down, and of being ungrateful, she knew with absolute certainty that she couldn't spend a minute longer in their house.

She had to get as far away from Almsford as possible, and then never look back. Somehow she needed to either get rid of her powers or avoid people so that there was no chance of ever hurting anyone ever again. She was far too dangerous, she understood now, to let people get close.

I have to be alone, she told herself. *I can't risk hurting anyone else.*

Once she was absolutely certain that everyone else in the house had gone to sleep, she very carefully opened the bedroom door and looked out onto the darkened landing. A window at the far end allowed just enough moonlight to fill the space, revealing that there was nobody lurking in any of the corners, so Lydia stepped out and made sure to avoid a few loose boards that she'd noted earlier. Holding her breath as much as possible, she crept to the top of the stairs and then began to make her way down; again, she'd checked on her way up earlier, and she knew as she walked down to the hallway that she needed to avoid the second, eighth and ninth steps.

Reaching the hallway, she hesitated again, just to rule out any last chance that someone might have waited up for her. In the back of her mind, she couldn't shake the feeling that Esme had given up a little too easily, that someone that smart and that precocious could never be fooled. Now, however, Lydia began to hope that she was going to enjoy just a little sprinkling of luck. After a few more seconds, she silently thanked the Walkers in her mind for their hospitality, and then she made her way through to the kitchen so that she could leave via the far less creaky back door.

The house remained silent for a few more seconds, before a floorboard on the landing creaked gently.

***

A fox cried out somewhere far off, its shriek briefly breaking the silence as Almsford slept under a blanket of stars.

Now that she'd walked around the corner, Lydia allowed herself to relax just a little. She was still so very thankful that she'd been able to get out of the cottage, and she wondered whether this might have been the Lord's way of telling her that she was right to leave. Then again, as she hurried along the next street, she couldn't help but wonder why the Lord would ever help her at all; she couldn't shake the fear that she was going to be struck down at any moment and then consigned to the fires of Hell, which – she supposed – was where she belonged.

Taking the next left, she quickly realized that she recognized this particular street. Only when she reached the other end, however, did she understand why: stopping near the corner, she found herself looking at Old Mother Marston's cottage.

This was where it had all begun.

Watching the dark upstairs windows, she

couldn't help but worry that at any moment she might spot an aged face peering out at her. She'd thought she'd seen such a thing once before, and she reasoned that an old woman with certain powers might easily find a way to linger after death. So far she saw no such face, yet she realized after a few more seconds that she felt strangely drawn to the house, as if some force wanted her to enter. A moment later, just as she was starting to convince herself that she must be wrong, she heard a faint cracking sound and watched as the dark little front door swung open to reveal a pitch-black interior.

And in that interior, barely visible, there stood a figure.

"No," Lydia said, instinctively taking a step back. "I want nothing to do with any of this."

"You have no choice," a voice replied, drifting out from inside Old Mother Marston's cottage. "I tried to warn you. Now there is only one option. You must learn to master your skills."

"No," Lydia said again, a little more firmly this time.

"I was like you once. I thought I knew better than anyone else. I cannot begin to describe the sorrow I felt when I realized the depths of my foolishness."

"I don't care," Lydia replied, once again feeling tears welling in her eyes. "This has nothing to do with me."

She turned to walk away.

"You will only know pain," the voice said, causing Lydia to stop in her tracks with her back still turned to the cottage, "and misery and shame. And loneliness. I see your life laid out before you, as easily as if you had unfolded a map. I see a shallow grave. I see a tight coffin. I see a young girl and her mother. I see you crawling out from the darkness and trying desperately to live."

"I don't *want* to live," Lydia said, and now tears were running freely down her face. "I would never fight for that, because I know I don't deserve to draw even one more breath. In fact..."

Her voice trailed off for a moment.

"In fact," she added, feeling a cold resolve running through her bones, "I'm going to prove you wrong. I'm not going to live a moment longer than I have to. These secrets I learned from your books... I shall take them to my grave, and I shall do that just as soon as I have worked out where I can die so that I shall never be found."

"You will live."

"I refuse," Lydia said through gritted teeth. "You'll see. I won't become like you."

She waited for a reply, for more mocking condescension, but a moment later she heard laughter instead. Turning, she looked at the cottage again, just as its front door slammed shut with such force that she worried the entire village might be woken.

She waited.

Silence.

Clenching her fists, she felt the urge to storm into the cottage and explain herself again, but part of her worried that this would merely prove to be a trap. Instead, relieved that the old woman was gone and half-convinced that she'd never really been there in the first place, Lydia turned and began to hurry once more along the street. Reaching the end, she stopped for a moment and tried to work out which way to go next. And then, just as she turned to head south across the village green, she heard the unmistakable sound of footsteps coming from somewhere over her shoulder.

"Going somewhere?"

Spinning round, she saw a figure silhouetted in the darkness. A moment later she realized that there were several other figures lurking nearby; and then the closest moved forward a little until Lydia was able to make out the face of the man who had recently offered to walk her to church.

"We have met before," he said gravely. "My name is Robert Potter."

"I don't mean to detain you," she replied, her voice trembling with fear. "I am merely -"

"Oh, I know what you are," he said, interrupting her as others began to form a circle around the spot where she was standing. "Believe me, Ms. Smith, I know *exactly* what you are. This fact has become quite clear to me over time."

"I'm leaving," she stammered, trying hard not to panic. "I won't trouble anyone in Almsford ever again. I won't set foot in the village after I'm gone."

"And why is that? Why do you fear this fine place and its good, honest people?"

"I don't," she continued, as she felt yet more tears starting to fill her eyes. Looking around, she realized that she was trapped, and now she knew she was going to have to make a dash for freedom. "I just want to leave, that's all."

"Then fly away!" Robert roared angrily. "Witch, you cannot deceive us, not now! We know what you are, and we are going to prove to the Lord that we shall not allow such evil to grow in our village!"

"Evil?"

She turned to him again.

"You're right," she said, "I'm truly evil. In fact, I'm so evil that -"

Before she could finish, she spotted another figure stepping out from behind Robert Potter. She opened her mouth to call out, but in that instant she saw Esme Walker glaring back at her.

"We have been informed," Robert sneered, "of the nature of your monstrous powers. That means we can avoid the lengthy waste of a trial and go straight to the punishment."

"It's exactly as I told you, Mr. Potter," Esme said, grinning as she kept her eyes fixed firmly on Lydia's horrified features. "I tricked her into confessing all her sins. I even managed to get her to show me some of her powers. I knew I was putting myself in the most horrid danger, but I was willing to sacrifice myself for the good of the village. I'm just so relieved that the witch has been rooted out now."

"Esme, no!" Lydia said, before taking a step back and looking around again. "I'm not a witch!" she shouted. "I just want to get out of here! You have to let me leave!"

In that moment she could no longer stop herself. She turned and ran, trying to slip between two of the women, but several hands quickly grabbed her from behind and dragged her down onto her knees, and soon fingernails were scratching at her body. A moment later Robert Potter stepped in front of her and placed the palm of a ragged, dirty hand against her face.

"Let all behold the true form of the witch as she struggles," he sneered as Lydia began to scream. "The time has come to cut her out of our lives forever!"

CHAPTER TWENTY-FIVE

THE FOLLOWING MORNING, AS sunlight began to spread across a lightening grayish sky, Lydia was still screaming. This time, however, she'd been chained to a small stool on the end of a wooden plank, and then she had been maneuvered past the riverbank so that she was suspended above the dirty water below.

All around, perhaps a hundred people – more or less the entire population of Almsford – had gathered to witness the execution.

"I am not a cruel man," Robert Potter called out loudly, watching from the other side of the river as Lydia struggled frantically to break free. "Never let it be claimed that I do not allow the course of justice to run as it must."

"Let me go!" Lydia shouted, pulling as hard as she could manage on the chains. Having spent the night tethered to a post in the village while being pelted with stones, she was scratched and bloodied all over. "Release me!"

"We must do this quickly," Robert continued, as Esme stood a little way behind him with a leery grin plastered across her face. "If we wait too long, the witch might use her powers against us."

"I'm not a witch!" Lydia screamed.

"I've told you everything I saw," Esme said, as saliva dribbled down her chin. Dropping to her knees, she seemed to be in an almost ecstatic thrall. "I made her show me!"

"Nobody here doubts you," Robert explained, as a murmur spread through the crowd.

"She's a liar!" Lydia sobbed, with tears gushing down her face as her bottom lip trembled violently. "She begged me to teach her things and I refused!"

"Never!" Esme gasped, pretending to be utterly shocked. "I can't listen to her vicious lies." With that, she clamped her hands over her ears and began to recite a prayer over and over again.

"Fortunately," Robert continued, "this fine young woman is not the only witness to Ms. Smith's wretched ways. The Lord has seen fit to deliver us another, one whose wisdom is beyond all reproach."

He kept his eyes fixed on Lydia for a few more seconds, before slowly turning to the gathered crowd.

"I shall prove to all of you that the Smith girl speaks with a forked tongue, and that the sins of our entire community can only be absolved if we act with speed!"

"Help me!" Lydia shouted, pulling so hard on the chains now that she could feel her bones starting to strain.

She jerked her head back, hitting the rickety board on the rear of the seat. A moment later, looking down, she saw the murky water of the river beneath her feet. Although she had been contemplating death before her capture, she had hoped to choose the manner of her own demise; now, faced with the prospect of more torture, she was filled with uncontrollable terror. More than anything, she hated the idea that her death might be taken as a victory for a bunch of murderous hypocrites.

"This isn't fair! I didn't do anything to any of you!" As more tears ran down her face, she looked across the river and spotted Esme staring back at her with a broader grin than ever. "You wanted my powers!" she yelled. "You were begging me to give you powers!"

She waited for a reply, but in that moment she merely felt as if she'd been played for a fool. Esme was watching her, clearly amused; a moment later, hearing the sound of a drumbeat approaching, Lydia turned and saw that several men were carrying some kind of cart toward the riverbank, and on that cart there sat a figure balanced delicately on a seat. Blinking away the tears, Lydia felt for a moment as if the sight made no sense at all, until finally she was able to see the figure's burned and bloodied features.

"What?" she whispered, still unable to quite understand what was happening. "I don't... what are you doing?"

Finally the cart stopped on the other side of the river, and the men took a few seconds to turn it around until the figure was facing the ducking stool. Lydia opened her mouth to call out again, to ask why she couldn't just be released, but at the very last second she saw the burned figure starting to move. Slowly, a sense of utter dread began to spread through her body. Although the figure had suffered horrific injuries, and looked more dead than alive, Lydia was starting to realize where she'd seen it before.

"The mother of Lydia Smith," Robert said solemnly, "is before us now. Mary Smith, a dutiful wife who only wanted the best for her family, was spared the ravages of the inferno at Bloodacre Farm for just long enough to join us today. I myself have counseled her in her agony since the flames cooked her body. She has clung to life purely because she knew she had a duty to be here today."

A murmur spread across the crowd, rippling in the cold morning air as gossip twisted and writhed from mouth to mouth.

"Amen," a voice said nearby.

"This poor woman's eyes are gone," Robert continued, "and her tongue too, and her lips. She hangs on in unbearable pain because she knows that this evil must be ripped from our community." He paused, keeping his gaze fixed on Lydia for a few more seconds before slowly turning and looking up at Mary's charred body on the cart. "Mary Smith," he announced, "the time has almost come for you to be released from your suffering. First, though, I beg of you that you might perform one last duty for the good people of Almsford. If there be a witch here, even if she be your own flesh and blood, you must point her out so that we can see her for what she truly is. Even without eyes, I am quite sure that you will be able to sense such a monstrosity."

"No," Lydia stammered, horrified by the sight of her mother's living corpse, unable to quite believe how such a thing could be possible at all. "Please..."

The crowd hushed, and a moment later Mary slowly began to raise her right hand. She was clearly struggling, as if Robert had been right when he'd claimed that she was barely clinging to life just so that she could reach this moment, but finally she extended one burned finger and pointed across the river, aiming directly at Lydia.

"No," Lydia said again, shaking her head as she saw the blood-filled pits that had once been her mother's eyes. "This can't be real. I can't -"

Suddenly Mary began to scream, shaking violently on the cart and spraying more blood from her mouth as she tried over and over again to say something. Still pointing at Lydia, she seemed convulsed by a great hatred that filled what remained of her body, shaking her violently as she somehow managed to keep pointing at her own daughter; although she had no eyes left, she seemed somehow to be still looking at Lydia, as if she knew the exact spot where her whimpering daughter sat chained to the ducking stool. More blood spluttered from her mouth, and as her rasping voice continued to spit out a series of furious gasps, everyone gathered at the riverbank began to understand the one word she was vainly trying again and again to scream.

"Witch!" a man shouted, followed by another, and then several women joined in as the word spread quickly across the gathered throng. "Witch! Witch! Witch!"

"Witch!" Robert Potter snarled, as even Esme joined in with the chant. "Mary Smith speaks the truth. After all, who else but a mother could ever know the truth about her own daughter?"

"WITCH!" a woman screamed, encouraging the others to raise their voices. "Kill the witch!"

"I'm not a witch!" Lydia cried out, even though deep down she knew they might all be right. "I didn't ask for any of this!"

On the cart, Mary Smith tried to rise to her feet. She almost succeeded, and for a few seconds – still pointing toward Lydia and trying to cry out – she managed to lift herself up slightly. The strain was clearly too much for her, however, and finally she let out one last cruel gurgle before slumping forward. Her dead body, finally drained of the hatred and venom that had somehow kept it alive since the fire, tumbled over the edge of the cart and slammed down lifelessly against the grass. Her huge gut burst open, spilling charred and rotten intestines across the ground. Maggots crawled out in their hundreds from the depths of her corpse.

"As the soul of Mary Smith rises to Heaven," Robert Potter pronounced, "we consign the soul of her daughter Lydia to the depths of Hell."

"No!" Lydia sobbed, as two men moved the wooden pin away from the rear of the ducking stool and grabbed the top section. "Somebody help me!"

"We leave the decision to the Lord!" Robert shouted as cries of 'WITCH!' became so loud that even his defiant voice risked being drowned out. "When we lift her back out of the water, if Lydia Smith has used her witchcraft to remain alive, then we shall know that the time has come to burn her! But if she dies, then we shall know that she had no powers at all, and that the Lord has taken her into His own embrace. There can be no fairer test than that, although I think we all know what is about to happen! Submerge this monstrous hag!"

"Wait!" Lydia shouted, pulling on the chains once more. "I only -"

Before she could finish, the stool crashed down. Still chained to the wooden seat, Lydia cried out one last time as she plunged beneath the river's surface. The stool, weighted down with chains and rocks, quickly slammed down against the riverbed, disturbing huge swirls of mud that burst up to fill the dark water. Still frantically trying to get free, Lydia screamed and screamed in the cold darkness, but already she could feel grit and dirt flooding into her nostrils, and after a few more seconds she began to take in great gulps of the river's filth. Unable to stop pulling against the chains, she looked up and saw a shimmering patch of light high above on the water's surface, with a few people starting to lean over so that they could look down at her. In that moment, drowning as more and more water flooded into her lungs, Lydia tried again to cry out, but all that emerged from her terrified mouth was a great rush of bubbles.

Finally she tried in vain to breathe, succeeding only in drawing water and sediment down her throat and into her dying body, threatening to burst her lungs open.

CHAPTER TWENTY-SIX

AS SOON AS THE bucket turned over, a rush of water gushed out, smashing against the muddy ground and washing away the worst of the dirt. Several chickens panicked and hurried toward the gate, and already the dirty water was forming pools and small rivers that ran away from the rear of the village's only inn.

"So here's what I don't understand," Maud Fisher said, wiping her brow as she set the bucket aside. "If Lydia Smith was a witch, then why didn't she try to save herself yesterday?"

"Mr. Potter thinks -"

"Oh, I heard what Mr. Potter thinks," Maud continued, turning to her sister Anne. "Believe me, nobody in Almsford could possibly not have heard that man's opinion several times over. He speaks it loudly enough on the village green whenever he gets the opportunity." She paused for a moment. "It's just that, when the Smith girl was brought back up, and when we all saw her wretched little corpse still chained in place, and that she'd drowned... by the rules Mr. Potter had mentioned just five or six minutes earlier, doesn't that mean that Lydia... *wasn't* a witch?"

"I admit that it's confusing," Anne replied, "but I think what Mr. Potter was trying to explain was that the girl was condemned either way. She certainly could have used her witchcraft to cling to life, but she also knew that the game was up. Everyone knew what she was. Even her own mother, in her final moments, condemned the girl to the flames of Hell. In that case, why wouldn't the witch accept defeat? Faced with our faith, she knew that death was her only option."

"I just feel like Mr. Potter changed the rules halfway through."

"It's not for us to question his methods, Maud. We're not privy to the same knowledge that he's got."

"But what if..."

Maud's voice trailed off for a few seconds.

"What if she's not really dead?" she asked finally. "What if, even now, she's using her powers to somehow... wait?"

"Well, that's why her corpse is strung up,

isn't it?" Anne said, before stepping past her sister and heading over to the corner of the building so that she could look toward the village green. "There's method in what Mr. Potter does, even if sometimes I don't quite understand it myself. I think we've got no choice here. We have to trust him."

Maud made her way over to join Anne, and for a moment both women looked toward the green. There, Lydia Smith's corpse hung from a noose that had been tied around its neck, for all the village to see. Silhouetted now against the gray sky, Lydia's dead body looked particularly pathetic, and a small group of people had already gathered to look up at it.

"Apparently it has to hang there until it's buried," Anne continued. "It's important, according to Mr. Potter, that everyone sees what happens to witches round these parts. It's also important to make sure that, like you suggested, she's not still playing some kind of game. You can never trust a witch. Even Mr. Potter admitted that much himself, he said that they're *always* playing tricks on decent folk. Fortunately, he knows what he's doing. We're lucky in Almsford that we've got men like him, men who can keep us safe."

"But what -"

"Hush!" Anne added, putting a finger against her lips as she turned to her sister. "You're full of questions this morning, aren't you? Just accept that there are some things we can't ever understand, and trust that there are others in our community who do that work for us. And be grateful, because not everyone's as lucky as us." She turned and headed back toward the yard. "Lydia Smith's dead. That's all we need to know."

Maud hesitated, watching as a few people walked past the distant hanging corpse while children played in the mud.

***

Picking up a rock, the young boy paused for a few seconds before launching the projectile, hitting Lydia's dangling body on the chest.

Laughing, the boy turned and ran away, desperate to get to safety lest the witch might wake up and use its powers.

Hanging from a branch of the oak tree, still wearing the same tattered dress, Lydia's corpse swung slightly as the wind picked up. The rope around its neck let out a faint creaking sound. Lydia's skin had become very pale now, and in some patches was starting to become an almost blue-green color. The corpse's matted hair hung down on either side of its face, and its eyes – slightly swollen and bloodshot from the all the time spent underwater – stared lifelessly at the muddy grass below. A fly briefly landed on one of the open eyes, crawling across from one lid to the other before making its way up a nostril.

The corpse's bare feet, caked in grit from the river, were hanging just low enough for another boy to leap up and touch the tips of the toes. The boy quickly ran away again to safety, joining his friends behind another tree, where they huddled for safety and laughed as they tried to come up with yet another game to play.

***

"I can't believe we invited such monstrous evil into our own home," Erica Walker said, her hand trembling slightly as she lit a candle in the cottage's kitchen. "How could I have been so stupid? How could I have been so easily fooled?"

"I knew something was wrong with that girl," Arthur replied darkly, sitting at the table and staring down at a plate of meat. "I felt it in my bones. When we went out to look at the ruins of Bloodacre Farm, we could all tell that whatever had happened out there... it wasn't natural."

"At least it's over now," Erica continued. "Mr. Potter's going to cut the witch down tomorrow morning and prepare her body for disposal. I don't know exactly what he's going to do with it, and I don't particularly care to find out. I just want this nightmare to be over."

"It should never have started in the first place," Arthur muttered, before turning as Esme stepped into the room. "Girl, you shouldn't have brought that witch to us. How stupid can you be?"

"I'm sorry, Father," Esme replied meekly. "She tried to seduce me with her powers. She wanted to tempt me to be like her, but I resisted. Doesn't that make me a good person?"

"It makes you weak for fraternizing with her in the first place," Arthur sneered. "How did I raise such a pathetic child?"

"I'm sorry, Father," Esme said, taking a seat at the table, barely able to meet her father's gaze. "It won't happen again."

"You're damn right it won't," Arthur told her. "Where have you been all afternoon, anyway?"

"I asked Mr. Potter if he could help me atone for my sins," Esme replied, reaching up to make sure that the collar of her dress was still covering the fresh cuts and scratches on one side of her neck. "I'm very grateful for his efforts. He took several hours to teach me the error of my ways."

"And did you learn anything?" Arthur asked.

"I did," Esme said, finally looking at him. She hesitated, struggling to hold back the pain, and after a few seconds she moved her hands down under the table so that they could no longer be seen. "Mr. Potter is a very good teacher. He's very...

thorough. I told him at the start, I begged him that he mustn't stop teaching me, not even if I cry out for help. He did what I wanted, and then more besides, and he even -"

"That's quite enough of such talk," Erica said firmly, setting a plate down firmly in front of her daughter. "We don't need to know the details, Esme. We just need to know that you'll be a little more thoughtful from now on."

"Oh, I will be," Esme said softly, looking down at the meat. "Mr. Potter thinks I might need a few more meetings with him, though, so I shall be going to see him again. I'm sure by the time he's finished with me, he'll have made sure that there's not so much as even a drop of doubt left anywhere in my body." She paused again, as her left eye twitched slightly. "Anywhere at all."

"Let us eat our meal in peace tonight," Arthur said after a moment as Erica took a seat to his left. "I for one have had enough of people talking incessantly over the past few days. Loose tongues are devilish things. There's something to be said for the virtue of remaining silent."

"I shall say grace," Erica replied, "and then I think you're right. Some quiet contemplation might be just what we all need after so much... unpleasantness."

As her mother began to say grace, Esme kept her eyes open. She slowly turned and looked at the window, and at the same time – under the table – she continued to use one ragged fingernail to cut into her left inner thigh, gradually working her way further up to meet the thicker marks that Robert Potter had carved into her earlier. She twisted the fingernail a little, trying to bring about the greatest pain possible, while thinking back to all the ways her teacher had cut and torn at her during their lesson. She remembered the agony he'd caused, and the way she'd had to fight so very hard, wriggling and writhing with her own hands clamped over her mouth in a desperate bid to remain silent.

And as those memories flooded through her body, with her mother still saying grace, Esme couldn't help but allow a smile to slowly creep across her lips. Already, a fresh bead of blood was dribbling down the inside of her left thigh.

CHAPTER TWENTY-SEVEN

"DO YOU NEED ANY assistance, Mr. Potter?" Luke Vance asked, standing in the doorway of the shed at the rear of the church. "I can stay, if you need me."

"That won't be necessary," Robert replied, still washing his hands in a bowl of water at the far end of the room. "You have done what I asked of you. Return now to your family and join them in prayer."

"But..."

For a moment, Luke could only stare at Lydia's corpse on the table. He'd helped cut it down and had carried it to the shed, but now he wondered whether he should stay to help a little more.

"Is it... safe?" he asked finally.

"Do you mean, am *I* safe?"

Turning to him with a smile, Robert hesitated before looking at Lydia's pale dead face.

"Yes, I'm quite safe," he continued. "The whole purpose of hanging this wretch on display was to show the people of Almsford that the witch poses no further threat. She can't hurt anyone ever again."

"But..." Luke paused, struggling with the logic. "If she drowned, doesn't that show that she *wasn't* a witch? A few people have been wondering about that part of the whole thing. It all seems a little... contradictory."

"Her demise went as intended," Robert continued, "and all good men can see that. There is no need to dig into the details. Even now, as we speak with her dead body between us, her soul is burning in the deepest, darkest fires of Hell. She can no longer cause any harm in this world." He stared at the side of Lydia's face for a moment, before turning to Luke. "Go to your family. Be safe. Be well."

"Of course," Luke replied, and now he sounded just a little relieved as he turned to hurry away.

"Oh, and Luke?" Robert called after him. "I hope to see all of your family at church on Sunday! Especially your sisters!"

Once he was alone, Robert took a deep breath and walked over to the side of the table. He looked once more at Lydia's face, before carefully reaching down and taking hold of the sides of her dress. He had to adjust his grip slightly, before finally ripping the fabric down the middle and pulling it away, then dropping what remained of the dress onto the floor.

"There," he said softly, with a smile. "You have no earthly possessions with you now. Just the flesh and blood with which you came into this world."

He turned to make his way over to the table, but at the last second he hesitated as he looked once more at Lydia's corpse. Its eyes were partially open, and after a moment he leaned down to get a better look at the pupils; he carefully rolled back the lid of the left eye, and he saw that the pupil was much larger than normal. Around the eye, meanwhile, blood vessels had burst in the pale grayish skin.

"The human body is a fascinating thing, is it not?" he continued. "I have always been interested in the way that it breaks down after death. The first twenty-four hours are the most interesting. There are so many changes, so many ways that the lack of blood-flow causes the body to start its disintegration. I have often thought that I should like to simply sit and watch for days on end while a body decomposes. There is, after all, such calmness in death."

He waited, letting the silence settle, still

looking into Lydia's dead eyes.

"Are you surprised that I am a man of science?" he asked. "I am first and foremost a man of faith, but I see no reason why science should not also interest me. After all, what is science but an expression of the Lord's creations in this world?"

Stepping over to one of the other benches, he picked up a knife and made his way back to Lydia's corpse. Kneeling down, he looked at the body's bare side and chose his spot carefully, before using the knife to gently cut a deep line through its flesh.

"No blood," he whispered, his voice tense with interest. "It congeals in you, does it not? It thickens and no longer flows through your veins."

He made another cut, forming a cross, and then he used a fingertip to pull aside one of the flaps of skin. He saw the glistening redness beneath, and when he dabbed a finger against that redness he was able to transfer some of the blood onto his own hand. Still, he knew full well that making such a cut on a live person would lead to much more spillage, and after a moment he pressed the back of his hand against Lydia's flesh, taking a few seconds to appreciate the lack of warmth.

"So beautiful," he purred. "I can *feel* the lack of a beating heart." He began to smear some of the stale blood down the corpse's side, toward its hip and then all the way to one of its knees. "It's like a cloak now, isn't it? It's like a cloak that you wore for your soul, but your soul is gone now so all that remains is this vestige of how you looked when you were alive." Suddenly filled with excitement, he got to his feet and hurried around to the top of the table, where he knelt again so that he could look more closely at Lydia's features. "Yet there is a difference," he added. "With all the muscles in your face relaxed, you *do* have a subtly altered appearance."

He ran the side of a finger against the body's cheek.

"Such a shame that your were drawn to darkness," he muttered. "You could have been a very good woman, and a good wife, had you just stayed on the right path. Then again, perhaps that is why you were drawn to darkness. You sensed your potential for purity and couldn't resist..."

His voice trailed off for a moment, before finally he got to his feet and took a couple of steps back.

"But I must remain strong," he added through gritted teeth. "There is temptation yet in this form, even though it be dead." He made the sign of the cross against his chest, before hurrying to one of the other tables. After taking one of the larger knives, he walked back over to Lydia's dead body. "There are just a few matters to attend to, and then -"

Before he could finish, he saw that both the eyes were wide open. He felt sure that they had not been so open just a few seconds earlier, yet now both eyes stared up at the ceiling as the candles continued to flicker nearby. Starting to doubt himself now, Robert thought back to the moment when he'd forced one of Lydia's eyes open; had he not then slid it shut again? And had the other eye not been mostly shut all along? Stepping around to the top of the table again, he looked down at the corpse's face and began to notice one other thing.

Had the muscles of Lydia's face not tightened slightly, almost as if they were returning her features to how they had been when she was alive? The change was subtle but impossible to miss.

"No," he whispered, even as he felt a sense of dread running through his body. "This is merely a test. The body changes even in death, that much I know. I must remain focused on the task at hand."

He paused for a few seconds, before pressing the knife's blade against one of Lydia's cheeks. Watching the dead girl's eyes carefully, he twisted the knife a little and began to cut a line down to the side of the mouth. No blood seeped from this latest fresh wound, of course, and in that moment Robert told himself that all his fears were simply another test from above.

"This is the wrong knife," he said, trying

desperately to get his head straight as he rushed to the other table and sorted through the various items, finally picking up a much smaller knife. Turning the blade around, he briefly spotted his own eyes reflected in the metal. "But *this* is the right one," he added firmly. "The Lord is watching over me. He knows that I am merely doing his bidding, and that I shall follow the path that is laid out before me."

Turning, he headed back over to the corpse. As he looked down at Lydia's body, however, he saw to his horror that a bead of blood was now running down from the cut on its face. Stepping around to the table's other side, he saw another bead running from the cross that he'd earlier made on the corpse's side; he tried to convince himself that this was merely an accident, but a moment later a second bead ran from the cut, followed by a third, almost as if...

Almost as if Lydia's blood was slowly starting to flow again.

A moment later a fat black fly scurried out from one of the girl's nostrils and flew away, buzzing around the room.

"This is not unusual," he said out loud, trying to convince himself of that fact. "I must simply cut some more signs into her flesh, to ward off evil spirits, and then my work here will be done. She can be buried properly once the proper protections are in place."

Stepping closer to the table, he reached down and – unable to steady his trembling hand – he struggled to cut a mark just below the body's belly button. He aimed to carve a symbol that he believed would promote purity, yet he froze as he saw fresh blood immediately starting to run from this latest wound. Looking over at Lydia's face, he let out a gasp as he realized that the eyes seemed now to have moved. They were no longer staring up at the ceiling and, instead, appeared to be looking at him directly.

"No!" he said firmly, turning his back to the sight, determined to regain control over his raging thoughts. Squeezing his eyes tight shut, he took a series of slow, deep breaths that gradually began to help a little. "Lord, give me the strength I require if I am to complete my work. Give me the faith that is needed if I am to prove myself. And above all, let your love shine down upon this place, so that nothing bad can happen here and only the righteous might prosper."

With his eyes still shut, he waited for some sign from above. Instead, after a few more seconds, he heard the unmistakable sound of a body – slightly stiff perhaps, and more than a little sore – sitting up on the table behind him.

CHAPTER TWENTY-EIGHT

SLOWLY OPENING HIS EYES, Robert Potter stared straight ahead, unable or unwilling to turn and see the figure that he now knew was sitting up on the table.

The fly, meanwhile, had landed on the far wall and was watching proceedings with interest.

"Lord," Robert whispered, still clutching the knife in his hands, "give me the strength to -"

"Look at me," Lydia said, cutting him off.

Robert immediately flinched.

"Why won't you look at me?" she continued, her voice sounding a little harsh and scratched. "Why won't you look upon your own work?"

After a moment, determined to prove his strength, Robert forced himself to turn. He immediately let out a horrified gasp and stepped back as he saw that Lydia was indeed sitting up and smiling at him. Already, some of the color seemed to be returning to her body.

"Isn't this what you wanted?" she asked calmly. "It is, isn't it? I can tell. I'm not the only one whose blood is flowing into unwarranted places."

"No," Robert stammered, and now it was his turn to look extremely pale as he shook his head. "This can't be happening."

"What's the matter?" she asked, before turning and climbing off the table, struggling slightly to stay on her feet once they were planted against the rough floorboards.

She reached out to steady herself against the side of the table for a few seconds, before standing up straight as she fully regained her balance.

"You wanted this. You foretold this. You announced to anyone who would listen that I was a... what's the word you used again? I thought it was such an ugly word at first, although I must admit that it's growing on me. Oh, yes, I remember now." She paused again. "Witch."

"No," Robert said again, before fumbling in his pocket for a moment and finally producing a silver crucifix. He quickly held the crucifix up in his shaking hand, as if he believed that he was now protected. "Get back from me!" he snarled. "The Lord commands that you leave me untouched!"

"Don't you think," Lydia replied, "that if the Lord had any involvement here at all, then we wouldn't have reached this point? I'm pretty sure that He would have stopped me long ago."

"I do not know how or why the Lord chooses to test my faith," Robert stammered. "Only that He does."

"I'm nobody's test, Mr. Potter," she said, stepping toward him. "I'm far more than that."

"Stay away from me!" he shouted, backing against the wall, still holding the crucifix up even though his hand was shaking more wildly than ever. "You cannot touch me!"

"Touch you?" Stopping in front of him, she hesitated for a moment. "Why would I *ever* want to touch you?" She paused, before reaching out and carefully taking the crucifix from his hand. "Although I could. If I wanted to, I could touch you all over."

"Be gone!" he sobbed, sinking to his knees as he looked up at her calm expression. "I beg the Lord to deliver me from this evil, so that I might continue His work!"

"The Lord has not, and *will* not, answer your prayers," she told him, before thinking for a few seconds. "However, I have my own master who has shown himself to be far more receptive. Don't you get it yet, Mr. Potter? Where your god offers nothing more than silence in the face of your prayers, my god delivers all that I could wish for and more."

"Never!"

"Then explain how I'm standing here now," she purred, "while you beg on your knees."

"I have faith!" he barked, before clutching his hands together and bowing his head. Closing his eyes tight, he took a series of deep, snatched breaths. "I pray to thee, Lord, that you will grant me the strength that I require in order to withstand this monstrosity that appears before me."

Lydia allowed a faint smile to reach her lips.

"I beseech thee," Robert continued, "to show me the righteous path that will lead me from this shadow and.... and..."

"What's wrong?" Lydia asked. "Are you running out of words?"

"Help me," Robert cried, and now tears were running from his tightly-shut eyes, cascading down his face. "Just help me, please..."

"He'd have helped you by now if He was going to," Lydia suggested. "Alternatively, you could pray to *my* master and I'm quite certain that your soul and spirit will be saved. Can you bring yourself to do that, Mr. Potter? You know my master's name, don't you? I'm sure you've lectured about such matters many times." She watched as he slumped down and began to whimper on the floor. "Pray to Satan, Mr. Potter," she snarled, "and you shall be saved. It's really that simple."

"Never!" he gasped.

"It's the only way to escape the immense pain that I can cause you," she added. "Let's start with fire. Don't you feel your flesh burning?"

"I cannot hear you!" he shouted. "I only -"

Suddenly letting out a cry, he pulled back and looked at his hands; the flesh was starting to bubble and char, as if burning in the intense heat of an invisible flame.

"Make it stop!" he shouted, his voice filled with a sense of panic. "Lord, save me!"

"I could burn you here and now," Lydia muttered, "but perhaps water would be a better way to end your miserable life."

Robert looked up at her, and in that moment he began to splutter and gasp. Clutching his throat, he tried to speak, but all that emerged from his lips was a series of cries as the skin all around his face began to shrink tighter against his skull.

"I'm taking all the water from your body," Lydia told him, "so that you'll be left as nothing more than a dehydrated husk." She watched as a gush of tears began to run down his cheeks. "Some parts of you will swell," she explained, "and some parts of you will dry out, and soon your body will become beset by the most unimaginable agony. I know it hurts now, Mr. Potter, but in the next few seconds you're going to experience a level of pain that has perhaps never been felt by any living thing in this world. Are you ready for that?"

"Please..."

"Yet you can stop it," she added, raising her eyebrows slightly. "It's really very easy. Just pray to *my* master, and you shall be returned to your ordinary, painless state."

"Never..."

"I don't think you have long left," she pointed out. "Can't you already feel the pain getting worse? Can't you feel the limitless potential of your body to experience the purest agony and -"

"Save me Satan!" he screamed suddenly, leaning forward and putting his arms around her waist, clutching her tightly as wretched sobs jerked his entire body. "Satan, help me! Save me from this pain!"

"Huh," Lydia whispered. "That was easier than I expected."

Gasping again, Robert fell down against the shed's wooden boards. As candles flickered nearby, their dancing light created ever-changing shadows across his hunched back as he struggled once more to get his breath back; finally he sat up again, looking straight ahead for a few seconds before lifting his gaze so that he could see Lydia staring back down at him. His mouth hung open, as if he was about to say something, yet no words left his lips; his eyes were drying now, although after a moment another solitary tear began to run down his left cheek.

"So much for your faith," Lydia sneered.

"I... I... I just..."

"I was only being silly, by the way," she continued. "I don't worship Satan. I never have and I never will. I just wanted to see how easily your faith could be torn down like... like an old wall that has served its purpose."

"I didn't... I mean, I never..."

"And it was very easy in the end, wasn't it?" she added. "You discarded your faith much faster than I ever expected. Perhaps it was never very strong to begin with."

Unable to complete a sentence, Robert looked down again, as if he truly couldn't believe that he'd actually begged Satan for help. Fresh tears were filling his eyes now, and after a few more seconds he reached up with his burned hands and touched the sides of his face.

"So we've tried fire," Lydia continued, "and we've tried water. However, I'm feeling as if I'm in an... imaginative mood this evening. So why don't we try the third of those wonderful elements?"

Robert hesitated, before looking up at her once more with eyes that were now bloodshot.

"Air," Lydia said softly. "Do you think you can be killed by air? Do you think I can find a way?"

"Forgive me," he said, shaking his head slowly in disbelief. He took a slow, deep breath. "I shall find a way to show my sorrow. I shall find a way to -"

Before he could finish, he let out a brief gulp. Furrowing his brow, he seemed confused by something, and a moment later he reached up and touched the edges of his mouth as he began to make a low wheezing sound.

"How does *that* feel?" Lydia asked, clearly amused by his suffering. "You can breathe in, but you can no longer breathe out. How does it feel to endlessly draw air into your lungs, with no way of expelling it again?"

Trying to speak, Robert clutched his throat. After a moment he stumbled to his feet, still gasping as he continued to suck air into his body. He began to claw at his own throat, as if trying to use his fingernails to dig fresh holes that might allow some of the air back out.

"It's such a natural thing, isn't it?" Lydia asked, watching with amusement as he stumbled across the room and leaned against the examination table. "There's nothing wrong with breathing in. It's so normal. We all do it so many times a day. But if you can't ever do the opposite, then what will happen?"

Still gasping frantically, Robert clambered onto the table and rolled onto his back. He was tearing at his throat now, while letting out a series of increasingly pained gulps.

"I suppose your lungs will fill and fill," Lydia mused, "until perhaps they'll burst." She watched as he arched his back and tilted his head to one side, as if he was still trying to find any way to force the air out. "You might suffocate before that. Or your body might react in some other, completely unexpected way as the pressure builds. I'm no physician, you see, so while I can do all of this... I have to watch and wait to see what the effect will be." She stepped over to the side of the table and looked down at his reddening face. Even now, he was still drawing air into his mouth and down into his lungs. "Is it wrong of me to find this so very fascinating?"

Now Robert began to bang the back of his head against the table, as if he was perhaps trying to shock the air out of his body. His gasps were changing every few seconds, becoming increasingly anguished, until eventually he fell entirely silent and his trembling stopped. For a couple of seconds longer he appeared to be entirely rigid, with his head tilting back, before finally his eyeballs bulged and popped out of their sockets, letting blood gush down the sides of his face. He twitched briefly, and then he fell still as more blood ran from the corners of his mouth.

"Well," Lydia said, staring down at him

impassively as a fly landed on his face, "that didn't *quite* end the way I expected."

CHAPTER TWENTY-NINE

THE WOODEN DOOR SLAMMED open with such force that it thudded against the wall and almost jumped off its hinges. A large, lumbering figure stepped into the darkened cabin and kicked the door shut, before dropping a heavy bag onto the floor and stumbling through the darkness.

After a moment, John Lord managed to light the solitary candle that stood on a small table next to his bed.

"Damn people," he sighed, crashing down onto the bed and rolling onto his back, looking up at the cabin's bare wooden ceiling as he struggled to get his breath back. Over the course of ten years he'd regained much of his earlier weight, but not as much muscle this time; instead he'd become profoundly huge, to the extent that sometimes he could barely breathe properly. "Always getting in the way," he continued. "Always poking their noses where they don't belong."

For the next few minutes, he simply lay on the bed and contemplated his miserable existence. He'd been busy all day, but now the light was starting to fade outside and he knew he faced yet another long night all alone. Sure, he had plenty of wine, and he knew that eventually he was going to start pouring much of that down his throat; the effort required to get up and go to the wine, however, felt like too much as he still struggled to get enough air into his lungs.

"This is why a man should have a wife," he said to himself. "They're only good for -"

Suddenly hearing a clicking sound nearby, he looked down toward the foot of the bed. A decade or so had passed since any other human being had set foot in John's cabin, yet for a day or so he'd begun to feel as if he was being watched. The cabin was filled with all sorts of junk that he'd collected over the years, and now John found himself watching the various boxes and sacks, waiting in case he spotted some sign of movement. He tried to focus on the fact that he was alone, yet now the sense of being watched felt stronger than ever. After a few seconds he looked at one particular old box and remembered how – many years earlier – he'd found some newborn kittens in there. He'd drowned the little bastards, dropping them into the river in a sack, and now he allowed himself a faint chuckle.

"You're losing your mind," he whispered, before leaning back again and staring at the ceiling, once more trying to summon the strength to get up and fetch some wine. "Man, you need to hold it all together. No good'll come of self-pity or paranoia."

He took another deep breath, and at last he felt as if he was finally feeling better.

"You're a loner," he added. "Always have been, and always will be. There's no point moaning about it, 'cause there's no-one who'll hear those moans and make it better. Everyone's on their own in the end. Might as well get used to that fact."

He paused, but now the lure of wine was too great. Bracing himself for the usual pain in his knees and back, he tried to get up from the bed, only to find that for some reason he couldn't move his body at all.

"What the..."

He tried again, then again, but somehow his limbs seemed to have frozen in place, almost as if the bones had fused together as nothing more than a series of thick metal poles. In fact, the harder he struggled to move, the more John felt as if he was locked solid, and finally he realized that he could barely move any part of himself at all. He could only look around, turning his eyeballs in their sockets as he tried to work out what was holding him down.

A moment later he felt something bumping against the bed, followed by some kind of creature gently brushing past his lower leg. Managing to look down, he heard a faint purring sound as he saw the tip of a black tail moving into sight. Puzzled, he tried to sit up, only to find that he still couldn't move properly.

And then a black cat stepped into view and climbed onto his chest, before stopping to look down into his eyes.

"What are..."

Barely able to move his lips, John stared up at the cat with a sense of genuine confusion.

"How did you get in here?" he gasped. "What's happening to me? Why can't I move?"

Smythe tilted his head slightly to one side, while still purring.

"I hate cats!" John hissed, trying in vain to knock the creature off but succeeding only in making his hefty chest shudder slightly. "I always have! You're nothing but vermin! Get out of here!"

He tried to shake the cat off again, but the only response was more purrs.

"What are you looking at me like that for?" John snarled. "Damn it, when I get up from here, you're in trouble! Do you know what happened to the last cats I got my hands on? I drowned them all in the river. Hell, even that was too merciful! I should've just stamped on their little heads and killed them that way!"

Suddenly Smythe stopped purring.

"What's up?" John sneered. "Feeling smug, are you? Enjoy it while you can, because any moment now I'm going to get up from this bed and rip you apart with my bare hands!" He struggled again, spluttering with frustration as he tried to turn first one way and then the other, still without any luck. "I don't know what's happening to me," he continued, straining every sinew in his body. "I've never felt like this before! I'm sure it's nothing, though. I'll be up in no time and then I'm going to make you pay!"

He strained for a few more seconds, until the effort became too much and he let out a heavy sigh. Exhausted, he looked up at the ceiling and told himself that he simply needed to regather his strength, and that after a minute or two more he'd be able to get back on his feet.

A moment later, however, Smythe leaned forward and looked down directly into John's eyes.

"Get out of here!" he yelled angrily. "You've got no right to be in my cabin! Go on, get out of here before I manage to get up and rip your head off your pathetic little body!"

Smythe hesitated for a moment, before leaning down and sniffing the side of John's cheek.

"What in God's name are you doing now?" John spluttered. "Have you lost your mind? Are you -"

Before he could finish, Smythe bit down hard on the flesh just to one side of his nose. Letting out a cry of pain, John instinctively tried to pull back, but he was powerless to resist as Smythe ripped the flesh away and started to chew. Blood quickly began to dribble down from the wound.

"Are you insane?" John gasped. "What the hell are you doing to me?"

Smythe continued to chew for a moment, before swallowing and then leaning down to rip another piece of flesh from John's face.

"Stop that!" John shouted. "Somebody help me!" he yelled, even though he knew there would be nobody around for miles to hear his cries. "I'm being attacked! Somebody get me out of here!"

With blood running from his mouth now, Smythe took a few seconds to chew this larger chunk of meat. He was still looking down at John, as if trying to decide what part of the man's face to eat next; once he'd leisurely swallowed his latest mouthful, he sniffed the gaping wound before ripping away an even larger strip, pulling off not only the top of John's cheek but also his lower eyelid. After letting out a howl of pain, John began to grunt as he tried yet again to haul himself up off the bed. Smythe, meanwhile, remained nonchalantly perched on the man's chest, seemingly unbothered by his struggles and focusing instead of the job of slowly but surely consuming his meal.

"Help me!" John yelled at the top of his voice. "Somebody get this vicious bastard off me!"

Smythe tilted his head again, as if amused by all the fuss. After a moment, however, the cat's eyes briefly filled with an unnatural redness, before he leaned down and bit harder than ever, sinking his fangs deep into John's cheek and eyeball before starting to rip them away with slow, firm force as he continued to eat the screaming man's face.

***

"Help me!" John's voice cried out, rising up high into the night sky. "Somebody -"

His latest cry twisted suddenly, as if he'd lost the ability to form words. His cabin was too far from civilization for anyone to hear his plaintive calls, of course. Had someone been close enough, then for the next few hours they might have heard the occasional spluttering gasp before – a little after midnight – the forest finally returned to silence.

CHAPTER THIRTY

AS MORNING SUNLIGHT STREAMED low across the fields, Lydia Smith walked barefoot away from Almsford. She was wearing her tattered dress, which just about covered her bruised and lacerated body. After sheltering in the shed for several hours with Robert Potter's corpse, she'd finally left as the sun had begun to rise, and to her relief she'd been able to get out of the village without running into anyone.

Now, with a cold morning wind blowing against her, she was stumbling slowly toward the crossroads ahead while trying to work out which direction to take. Part of her, meanwhile, just wanted to settle down on the ground and close her eyes and never -

"Lydia!"

Stopping, she felt for a moment that she must have imagined that voice. She half-turned, and she felt a flicker of dread running through her chest as she saw Esme Walker hurrying to catch up.

"Lydia," Esme continued breathlessly, stopping and putting a hand on the side of her arm, "where -"

"Don't touch me!" Lydia gasped, pulling away.

"I'm sorry, Lydia," Esme continued excitedly. "Where are you going? I thought..."

She looked her up and down for a moment, clearly in shock, before breaking into a smile.

"I knew it!" she shouted. "I knew you weren't really dead! Everyone was talking about how you'd been drowned, and then when you were hanging from the tree in the village square I actually thought it might have all gone wrong, but I always had this glimmer of hope in my heart that you were going to be fine!"

She stepped forward and put her arms around Lydia, hugging her tight.

"I knew -"

"Don't touch me!" Lydia snarled, pulling back and this time shoving Esme so hard that she almost knocked the girl over. "Do that again and I'll..."

As her voice trailed off, she realized that she wasn't quite sure what she'd do if Esme continued to touch her, but she knew she'd find some way to make her stop.

"I get it," Esme continued, before letting out a sigh. "Listen, I only said those awful things when you were in the ducking stool because... I suppose I was angry. I was angry at you for not sharing your gift, but we can put that all behind us now, can't we? I completely forgive you. Robert Potter's dead, and that means you're free. You can be what you want to be, *where* you want to be, and I can come with you and sort of be your familiar and you can teach me things." She paused, waiting for an answer. "In your own time, of course," she added. "I'd never want to pressure you."

Lydia opened her mouth to reply, but for a moment she really wasn't quite sure what to say. Something about Esme just seemed so utterly... ridiculous.

"We can be a team," Esme suggested, and now she sounded just a little desperate. "You'll be in charge, obviously, but I know I can help out here and there. Please, Lydia, won't you just let me come? I don't even have to go back to the village and say goodbye to Mother and Father, I can leave with you right now!" She pulled a pouch from her pocket and held it out, before setting it down in front of Lydia's feet. "I took this gold from Father's secret stash," she continued. "There are some jewels in there, too. I don't think he even understood their value, but they can help us get started. We might even have enough to buy a house of our own!"

"How did you know?" Lydia asked.

"How did I know what?"

"That Robert Potter's dead."

"Because I watched you kill him," Esme replied, before rolling her eyes. "I was looking through a gap in the wall, Lydia. I saw it all. I saw him stripping you down, and I saw him cutting you. I can't even begin to tell you how much my heart was pounding, but I still held onto this scrap of hope that you were going to get up and make him pay. And you did! Watching what you did to him... it was extraordinary!"

"You were watching the whole time?" Lydia asked, before furrowing her brow. "I suppose I shouldn't be surprised. You and your family are sneaky like that, aren't you?"

"He deserved everything he got," Esme said firmly. "Now we're *both* free, Lydia. I can't even begin to tell you all the things that Mr. Potter used to do to me. He always called himself a man of the Lord but, well, he could get very nasty at times. Sometimes he went too far for my liking." She reached out, taking hold of Lydia's hands and squeezing them tight. "I can't wait to find out what adventures we'll have," she continued. "Oh Lydia, do you realize how much fun is waiting out there for us in the world? With your powers, and with the powers you'll eventually teach me whenever you're ready, we can do anything!"

"You're touching me again," Lydia replied, trying to pull away, only to find that Esme's grip was too tight this time. "I don't like being touched. And I want to be alone."

"So where shall we go first?" Esme asked, her eyes shining with anticipation. "Do you have somewhere in mind? We could go and cause trouble in one of the other villages. That would be so much fun! Or we could go somewhere a little bigger, perhaps somewhere by the sea, like Folkestone or Crowford. Or we could go to London! But we need to be careful, because we don't want to attract too much attention. I'm sure there are plenty of other men out there like Mr. Potter who'd be only too happy to... well, you know what I mean. But do you have a place in mind? Tell me you do, Lydia! Tell me where we're going!"

"You're touching me," Lydia sneered darkly under her breath.

"I think we should go to the sea," Esme explained. "Let's start out small and see what we can get away with. I bet you'll soon find that it's useful if I can do a few tricks and I'm really a very good learner. Father's always telling me that, he says I'm really a very clever girl and that I'm almost too intelligent for my own good. He often says that I'll never get myself a decent husband if I don't learn to keep my mouth shut a little more, but I'm not sure whether he really means that. Anyway, we can find out together what we're capable of achieving. It'll just be you and me, Lydia. You and me forever. What do you think about that idea?"

"You're touching me," Lydia said again, though gritted teeth.

"Oh, sorry," Esme replied, chuckling but not releasing her grip. "Listen, how about -"

"Stop touching me!" Lydia screamed, suddenly pushing Esme back and forcing her down onto her knees in the mud. "Why won't you stop touching me?"

"I'm sorry!" Esme gasped. "I just -"

Before she could finish, she gasped again. Reaching up, she touched her throat, and now her eyes were almost bulging from their sockets.

"Why won't people ever listen to me?" Lydia continued. "I want to be left alone, I want to be ignored, and I don't want anyone to ever touch me again!"

"I understand!" Esme hissed, struggling to breathe as she stayed down on her knees. "I always understood! Lydia, please..."

As Esme struggled desperately for breath, Lydia watched her suffering and wondered whether she could simply kill her. After all, she'd already killed not only Robert Potter but also her own father, and she supposed that she could visit the same fate upon Esme now. Already she could feel the temptation growing, and she thought of Esme suffering the same fate as Mr. Potter, of her eyeballs slowly getting squeezed from their sockets and her whole body starting to burst...

That idea felt so good, yet at the same time Lydia also wondered whether Esme was worth the effort. Killing Mr. Potter had taken several minutes but had exhausted her so much that she'd been unable to walk away from the shed for a number of hours. Now, as Esme's eyes began very slowly to bulge, Lydia realized that perhaps she needed to show a little more mercy.

"Please," Esme stammered, reaching a hand out, "make it slower."

Lydia tilted her head, trying to understand.

"I like it slow," Esme said, grinning as her eyes bulged even more. "I like it so slow and so tender, and so sensual..."

She touched Lydia's hand again.

"I like it slow and -"

In that instant, Lydia flinched. Losing control for a fraction of a second, she watched as Esme's head burst open with huge force. As blood sprayed across her face and chest, Lydia saw Esme's body still kneeling before her with only a bloodied stump for a neck. After a few more seconds, the corpse tilted to one side and finally fell down dead against the ground, splattering wet mud across

Lydia's bare feet.

"Huh," Lydia said softly. "That didn't go the way I expected either."

She stood in silence for a moment, before turning to walk away. Stopping, she saw the pouch on the ground; she picked it up and looked inside, and sure enough she found some jewelry and gold coins. The idea that Esme's father had such a pouch sitting around seemed unlikely, but she remembered reading some spells out loud, and a few of them had mentioned riches; she supposed that one of those spells might have conjured the pouch and sent it in her direction. And she was no expert, but she reasoned that this should be enough to allow her to buy a new home somewhere, so she slipped the pouch into her pocket and then walked to the crossroads. And then, as she got there, she saw a small dark shape emerging from the long grass on the other side of the road.

"Smythe!" she stammered, before rushing over and kneeling down to stroke him. "You found me! But... how? Where have you been?"

Purring, Smythe brushed against her.

She smiled.

"Is that blood around your mouth?" she asked, wiping some of the blood away. "You look well-fed, too. I thought you'd abandoned me forever."

Turning and flicking his tail, Smythe

pressed against her with his other side.

"You have no idea what's been going on," she continued, before getting to her feet. "You wouldn't even believe me if I told you." She looked first one way and then the other. "We can't stay around here," she explained. "It's just not possible. Too many people know too much. We need to go to some new place where nobody has ever heard of us before. Well, of *me*, at least." She looked down. "Do you want to come?"

Smythe met her gaze and let out a loud meowing sound.

"Okay," Lydia said, before spotting a patch of sunlight at the far end of the road to her right. She paused, and then she set off in that direction with Smythe walking alongside, both of them heading toward the horizon. "We'll try this way. I truly don't know where we'll end up, but... I think we should just have a little faith, and trust that the Lord will send us along the right path."

Next in this series

THE HORROR OF STYRE HOUSE
(THE SMYTHE TRILOGY BOOK 3)

Lydia Smith thinks she has finally escaped from her tragic past. Living a quiet, contented life with her familiar Smythe, she hopes to avoid any trouble.

But when whispers start to spread and the local villagers learn about Lydia's mysterious books, she realizes that she might never be free.

Soon Lydia comes up with a plan. She knows she's doomed, but she's determined to find some way to outlive her own failing body. The books offer a solution, albeit one that comes at a terrible cost.

Although she always promised herself that she'd never use her powers for evil, Lydia finds herself pushed to breaking point.

As angry villagers close in, will she commit the ultimate sin in a desperate attempt to survive?

AMY CROSS

Also by Amy Cross

1689
(The Haunting of Hadlow House book 1)

All Richard Hadlow wants is a happy family and a peaceful home. Having built the perfect house deep in the Kent countryside, now all he needs is a wife. He's about to discover, however, that even the most perfectly-laid plans can go horribly and tragically wrong.

The year is 1689 and England is in the grip of turmoil. A pretender is trying to take the throne, but Richard has no interest in the affairs of his country. He only cares about finding the perfect wife and giving her a perfect life. But someone – or something – at his newly-built house has other ideas. Is Richard's new life about to be destroyed forever?

Hadlow House is brand new, but already there are strange whispers in the corridors and unexplained noises at night. Has Richard been unlucky, is his new wife simply imagining things, or is a dark secret from the past about to rise up and deliver Richard's worst nightmare?
Who wins when the past and the present collide?

Also by Amy Cross

The Haunting of Nelson Street
(The Ghosts of Crowford book 1)

Crowford, a sleepy coastal town in the south of England, might seem like an oasis of calm and tranquility. Beneath the surface, however, dark secrets are waiting to claim fresh victims, and ghostly figures plot revenge.

Having finally decided to leave the hustle of London, Daisy and Richard Johnson buy two houses on Nelson Street, a picturesque street in the center of Crowford. One house is perfect and ready to move into, while the other is a fire-ravaged wreck that needs a lot of work. They figure they have plenty of time to work on the damaged house while Daisy recovers from a traumatic event.

Soon, they discover that the two houses share a common link to the past. Something awful once happened on Nelson Street, something that shook the town to its core.

Also by Amy Cross

The Revenge of the Mercy Belle
(The Ghosts of Crowford book 2)

The year is 1950, and a great tragedy has struck the town of Crowford. Three local men have been killed in a storm, after their fishing boat the Mercy Belle sank. A mysterious fourth man, however, was rescue. Nobody knows who he is, or what he was doing on the Mercy Belle... and the man has lost his memory.

Five years later, messages from the dead warn of impending doom for Crowford. The ghosts of the Mercy Belle's crew demand revenge, and the whole town is being punished. The fourth man still has no memory of his previous existence, but he's married now and living under the named Edward Smith. As Crowford's suffering continues, the locals begin to turn against him.

What really happened on the night the Mercy Belle sank? Did the fourth man cause the tragedy? And will Crowford survive if this man is not sent to meet his fate?

Also by Amy Cross

The Devil, the Witch and the Whore
(The Deal book 1)

"Leave the forest alone. Whatever's out there, just let it be. Don't make it angry."

When a horrific discovery is made at the edge of town, Sheriff James Kopperud realizes the answers he seeks might be waiting beyond in the vast forest. But everybody in the town of Deal knows that there's something out there in the forest, something that should never be disturbed. A deal was made long ago, a deal that was supposed to keep the town safe. And if he insists on investigating the murder of a local girl, James is going to have to break that deal and head out into the wilderness.

Meanwhile, James has no idea that his estranged daughter Ramsey has returned to town. Ramsey is running from something, and she thinks she can find safety in the vast tunnel system that runs beneath the forest. Before long, however, Ramsey finds herself coming face to face with creatures that hide in the shadows. One of these creatures is known as the devil, and another is known as the witch. They're both waiting for the whore to arrive, but for very different reasons. And soon Ramsey is offered a terrible deal, one that could save or destroy the entire town, and maybe even the world.

Also by Amy Cross

If You Didn't Like Me Then, You Probably Won't Like Me Now

One year ago, Sheryl and her friends did something bad. Really bad. They ritually humiliated local girl Rachel Ritter, before posting the video online for all to see. After that night, Rachel left town and was never seen again. Until now.

Late one night, Sheryl and her friends realize that Rachel's back. At first they think there's on reason to be concerned, but a series of strange events soon convince them that they need to be worried. On the outside, Rachel acts as if all is forgiven, but she's hiding a shocking secret that soon starts to have deadly consequences.

By the time they understand the full horror of Rachel's plans, Sheryl and her friends might be too late to save themselves. Is Rachel really out for revenge? What does she have in store for her tormentors? And just how far is she willing to go? Would she, for example, do something that nobody in all of human history has ever managed to achieve?

If You Didn't Like Me Then, You Probably Won't Like Me Now is a horror novel about the surprising nature of revenge, about the power of hatred, and about the future of humanity.

Also by Amy Cross

The Soul Auction

"I saw a woman on the beach. I watched her face a demon."

Thirty years after her mother's death, Alice Ashcroft is drawn back to the coastal English town of Curridge. Somebody in Curridge has been reviewing Alice's novels online, and in those reviews there have been tantalizing hints at a hidden truth. A truth that seems to be linked to her dead mother.

"Thirty years ago, there was a soul auction."

Once she reaches Curridge, Alice finds strange things happening all around her. Something attacks her car. A figure watches her on the beach at night. And when she tries to find the person who has been reviewing her books, she makes a horrific discovery.

What really happened to Alice's mother thirty years ago? Who was she talking to, just moments before dropping dead on the beach? What caused a huge rockfall that nearly tore a nearby cliff-face in half? And what sinister presence is lurking in the grounds of the local church?

Also by Amy Cross

The Ash House

Why would anyone ever return to a haunted house?

For Diane Mercer the answer is simple. She's dying of cancer, and she wants to know once and for all whether ghosts are real.

Heading home with her young son, Diane is determined to find out whether the stories are real. After all, everyone else claimed to see and hear strange things in the house over the years. Everyone except Diane had some kind of experience in the house, or in the little ash house in the yard.

As Diane explores the house where she grew up, however, her son is exploring the yard and the forest. And while his mother might be struggling to come to terms with her own impending death, Daniel Mercer is puzzled by fleeting appearances of a strange little girl who seems drawn to the ash house, and by strange, rasping coughs that he keeps hearing at night.

The Ash House is a horror novel about a woman who desperately wants to know what will happen to her when she dies, and about a boy who uncovers the shocking truth about a young girl's murder.

Also by Amy Cross

Haunted

Twenty years ago, the ghost of a dead little girl drove Sheriff Michael Blaine to his death.

Now, that same ghost is coming for his daughter.

Returning to the small town where she grew up, Alex Roberts is determined to live a normal, quiet life. For the residents of Railham, however, she's an unwelcome reminder of the town's darkest hour.

Twenty years ago, nine-year-old Mo Garvey was found brutally murdered in a nearby forest. Everyone thinks that Alex's father was responsible, but if the killer was brought to justice, why is the ghost of Mo Garvey still after revenge?

And how far will the real killer go to protect his secret, when Alex starts getting closer to the truth?

Haunted is a horror novel about a woman who has to face her past, about a town that would rather forget, and about a little girl who refuses to let death stand in her way.

AMY CROSS

Also by Amy Cross

The Curse of Wetherley House

"If you walk through that door, Evil Mary will get you."

When she agrees to visit a supposedly haunted house with an old friend, Rosie assumes she'll encounter nothing more scary than a few creaks and bumps in the night. Even the legend of Evil Mary doesn't put her off. After all, she knows ghosts aren't real. But when Mary makes her first appearance, Rosie realizes she might already be trapped.

For more than a century, Wetherley House has been cursed. A horrific encounter on a remote road in the late 1800's has already caused a chain of misery and pain for all those who live at the house. Wetherley House was abandoned long ago, after a terrible discovery in the basement, something has remained undetected within its room. And even the local children know that Evil Mary waits in the house for anyone foolish enough to walk through the front door.

Before long, Rosie realizes that her entire life has been defined by the spirit of a woman who died in agony. Can she become the first person to escape Evil Mary, or will she fall victim to the same fate as the house's other occupants?

AMY CROSS

BOOKS BY AMY CROSS

1. Dark Season: The Complete First Series (2011)
2. Werewolves of Soho (Lupine Howl book 1) (2012)
3. Werewolves of the Other London (Lupine Howl book 2) (2012)
4. Ghosts: The Complete Series (2012)
5. Dark Season: The Complete Second Series (2012)
6. The Children of Black Annis (Lupine Howl book 3) (2012)
7. Destiny of the Last Wolf (Lupine Howl book 4) (2012)
8. Asylum (The Asylum Trilogy book 1) (2012)
9. Dark Season: The Complete Third Series (2013)
10. Devil's Briar (2013)
11. Broken Blue (The Broken Trilogy book 1) (2013)
12. The Night Girl (2013)
13. Days 1 to 4 (Mass Extinction Event book 1) (2013)
14. Days 5 to 8 (Mass Extinction Event book 2) (2013)
15. The Library (The Library Chronicles book 1) (2013)
16. American Coven (2013)
17. Werewolves of Sangreth (Lupine Howl book 5) (2013)
18. Broken White (The Broken Trilogy book 2) (2013)
19. Grave Girl (Grave Girl book 1) (2013)
20. Other People's Bodies (2013)
21. The Shades (2013)
22. The Vampire's Grave and Other Stories (2013)
23. Darper Danver: The Complete First Series (2013)
24. The Hollow Church (2013)
25. The Dead and the Dying (2013)
26. Days 9 to 16 (Mass Extinction Event book 3) (2013)
27. The Girl Who Never Came Back (2013)
28. Ward Z (The Ward Z Series book 1) (2013)
29. Journey to the Library (The Library Chronicles book 2) (2014)
30. The Vampires of Tor Cliff Asylum (2014)
31. The Family Man (2014)
32. The Devil's Blade (2014)
33. The Immortal Wolf (Lupine Howl book 6) (2014)
34. The Dying Streets (Detective Laura Foster book 1) (2014)
35. The Stars My Home (2014)
36. The Ghost in the Rain and Other Stories (2014)
37. Ghosts of the River Thames (The Robinson Chronicles book 1) (2014)
38. The Wolves of Cur'eath (2014)
39. Days 46 to 53 (Mass Extinction Event book 4) (2014)
40. The Man Who Saw the Face of the World (2014)
41. The Art of Dying (Detective Laura Foster book 2) (2014)
42. Raven Revivals (Grave Girl book 2) (2014)

43. Arrival on Thaxos (Dead Souls book 1) (2014)
44. Birthright (Dead Souls book 2) (2014)
45. A Man of Ghosts (Dead Souls book 3) (2014)
46. The Haunting of Hardstone Jail (2014)
47. A Very Respectable Woman (2015)
48. Better the Devil (2015)
49. The Haunting of Marshall Heights (2015)
50. Terror at Camp Everbee (The Ward Z Series book 2) (2015)
51. Guided by Evil (Dead Souls book 4) (2015)
52. Child of a Bloodied Hand (Dead Souls book 5) (2015)
53. Promises of the Dead (Dead Souls book 6) (2015)
54. Days 54 to 61 (Mass Extinction Event book 5) (2015)
55. Angels in the Machine (The Robinson Chronicles book 2) (2015)
56. The Curse of Ah-Qal's Tomb (2015)
57. Broken Red (The Broken Trilogy book 3) (2015)
58. The Farm (2015)
59. Fallen Heroes (Detective Laura Foster book 3) (2015)
60. The Haunting of Emily Stone (2015)
61. Cursed Across Time (Dead Souls book 7) (2015)
62. Destiny of the Dead (Dead Souls book 8) (2015)
63. The Death of Jennifer Kazakos (Dead Souls book 9) (2015)
64. Alice Isn't Well (Death Herself book 1) (2015)
65. Annie's Room (2015)
66. The House on Everley Street (Death Herself book 2) (2015)
67. Meds (The Asylum Trilogy book 2) (2015)
68. Take Me to Church (2015)
69. Ascension (Demon's Grail book 1) (2015)
70. The Priest Hole (Nykolas Freeman book 1) (2015)
71. Eli's Town (2015)
72. The Horror of Raven's Briar Orphanage (Dead Souls book 10) (2015)
73. The Witch of Thaxos (Dead Souls book 11) (2015)
74. The Rise of Ashalla (Dead Souls book 12) (2015)
75. Evolution (Demon's Grail book 2) (2015)
76. The Island (The Island book 1) (2015)
77. The Lighthouse (2015)
78. The Cabin (The Cabin Trilogy book 1) (2015)
79. At the Edge of the Forest (2015)
80. The Devil's Hand (2015)
81. The 13th Demon (Demon's Grail book 3) (2016)
82. After the Cabin (The Cabin Trilogy book 2) (2016)
83. The Border: The Complete Series (2016)
84. The Dead Ones (Death Herself book 3) (2016)
85. A House in London (2016)
86. Persona (The Island book 2) (2016)

87. Battlefield (Nykolas Freeman book 2) (2016)
88. Perfect Little Monsters and Other Stories (2016)
89. The Ghost of Shapley Hall (2016)
90. The Blood House (2016)
91. The Death of Addie Gray (2016)
92. The Girl With Crooked Fangs (2016)
93. Last Wrong Turn (2016)
94. The Body at Auercliff (2016)
95. The Printer From Hell (2016)
96. The Dog (2016)
97. The Nurse (2016)
98. The Haunting of Blackwych Grange (2016)
99. Twisted Little Things and Other Stories (2016)
100. The Horror of Devil's Root Lake (2016)
101. The Disappearance of Katie Wren (2016)
102. B&B (2016)
103. The Bride of Ashbyrn House (2016)
104. The Devil, the Witch and the Whore (The Deal Trilogy book 1) (2016)
105. The Ghosts of Lakeforth Hotel (2016)
106. The Ghost of Longthorn Manor and Other Stories (2016)
107. Laura (2017)
108. The Murder at Skellin Cottage (Jo Mason book 1) (2017)
109. The Curse of Wetherley House (2017)
110. The Ghosts of Hexley Airport (2017)
111. The Return of Rachel Stone (Jo Mason book 2) (2017)
112. Haunted (2017)
113. The Vampire of Downing Street and Other Stories (2017)
114. The Ash House (2017)
115. The Ghost of Molly Holt (2017)
116. The Camera Man (2017)
117. The Soul Auction (2017)
118. The Abyss (The Island book 3) (2017)
119. Broken Window (The House of Jack the Ripper book 1) (2017)
120. In Darkness Dwell (The House of Jack the Ripper book 2) (2017)
121. Cradle to Grave (The House of Jack the Ripper book 3) (2017)
122. The Lady Screams (The House of Jack the Ripper book 4) (2017)
123. A Beast Well Tamed (The House of Jack the Ripper book 5) (2017)
124. Doctor Charles Grazier (The House of Jack the Ripper book 6) (2017)
125. The Raven Watcher (The House of Jack the Ripper book 7) (2017)
126. The Final Act (The House of Jack the Ripper book 8) (2017)
127. Stephen (2017)
128. The Spider (2017)
129. The Mermaid's Revenge (2017)
130. The Girl Who Threw Rocks at the Devil (2018)

131. Friend From the Internet (2018)
132. Beautiful Familiar (2018)
133. One Night at a Soul Auction (2018)
134. 16 Frames of the Devil's Face (2018)
135. The Haunting of Caldgrave House (2018)
136. Like Stones on a Crow's Back (The Deal Trilogy book 2) (2018)
137. Room 9 and Other Stories (2018)
138. The Gravest Girl of All (Grave Girl book 3) (2018)
139. Return to Thaxos (Dead Souls book 13) (2018)
140. The Madness of Annie Radford (The Asylum Trilogy book 3) (2018)
141. The Haunting of Briarwych Church (Briarwych book 1) (2018)
142. I Just Want You To Be Happy (2018)
143. Day 100 (Mass Extinction Event book 6) (2018)
144. The Horror of Briarwych Church (Briarwych book 2) (2018)
145. The Ghost of Briarwych Church (Briarwych book 3) (2018)
146. Lights Out (2019)
147. Apocalypse (The Ward Z Series book 3) (2019)
148. Days 101 to 108 (Mass Extinction Event book 7) (2019)
149. The Haunting of Daniel Bayliss (2019)
150. The Purchase (2019)
151. Harper's Hotel Ghost Girl (Death Herself book 4) (2019)
152. The Haunting of Aldburn House (2019)
153. Days 109 to 116 (Mass Extinction Event book 8) (2019)
154. Bad News (2019)
155. The Wedding of Rachel Blaine (2019)
156. Dark Little Wonders and Other Stories (2019)
157. The Music Man (2019)
158. The Vampire Falls (Three Nights of the Vampire book 1) (2019)
159. The Other Ann (2019)
160. The Butcher's Husband and Other Stories (2019)
161. The Haunting of Lannister Hall (2019)
162. The Vampire Burns (Three Nights of the Vampire book 2) (2019)
163. Days 195 to 202 (Mass Extinction Event book 9) (2019)
164. Escape From Hotel Necro (2019)
165. The Vampire Rises (Three Nights of the Vampire book 3) (2019)
166. Ten Chimes to Midnight: A Collection of Ghost Stories (2019)
167. The Strangler's Daughter (2019)
168. The Beast on the Tracks (2019)
169. The Haunting of the King's Head (2019)
170. I Married a Serial Killer (2019)
171. Your Inhuman Heart (2020)
172. Days 203 to 210 (Mass Extinction Event book 10) (2020)
173. The Ghosts of David Brook (2020)
174. Days 349 to 356 (Mass Extinction Event book 11) (2020)

175. The Horror at Criven Farm (2020)
176. Mary (2020)
177. The Middlewych Experiment (Chaos Gear Annie book 1) (2020)
178. Days 357 to 364 (Mass Extinction Event book 12) (2020)
179. Day 365: The Final Day (Mass Extinction Event book 13) (2020)
180. The Haunting of Hathaway House (2020)
181. Don't Let the Devil Know Your Name (2020)
182. The Legend of Rinth (2020)
183. The Ghost of Old Coal House (2020)
184. The Root (2020)
185. I'm Not a Zombie (2020)
186. The Ghost of Annie Close (2020)
187. The Disappearance of Lonnie James (2020)
188. The Curse of the Langfords (2020)
189. The Haunting of Nelson Street (The Ghosts of Crowford 1) (2020)
190. Strange Little Horrors and Other Stories (2020)
191. The House Where She Died (2020)
192. The Revenge of the Mercy Belle (The Ghosts of Crowford 2) (2020)
193. The Ghost of Crowford School (The Ghosts of Crowford book 3) (2020)
194. The Haunting of Hardlocke House (2020)
195. The Cemetery Ghost (2020)
196. You Should Have Seen Her (2020)
197. The Portrait of Sister Elsa (The Ghosts of Crowford book 4) (2021)
198. The House on Fisher Street (2021)
199. The Haunting of the Crowford Hoy (The Ghosts of Crowford 5) (2021)
200. Trill (2021)
201. The Horror of the Crowford Empire (The Ghosts of Crowford 6) (2021)
202. Out There (The Ted Armitage Trilogy book 1) (2021)
203. The Nightmare of Crowford Hospital (The Ghosts of Crowford 7) (2021)
204. Twist Valley (The Ted Armitage Trilogy book 2) (2021)
205. The Great Beyond (The Ted Armitage Trilogy book 3) (2021)
206. The Haunting of Edward House (2021)
207. The Curse of the Crowford Grand (The Ghosts of Crowford 8) (2021)
208. How to Make a Ghost (2021)
209. The Ghosts of Crossley Manor (The Ghosts of Crowford 9) (2021)
210. The Haunting of Matthew Thorne (2021)
211. The Siege of Crowford Castle (The Ghosts of Crowford 10) (2021)
212. Daisy: The Complete Series (2021)
213. Bait (Bait book 1) (2021)
214. Origin (Bait book 2) (2021)
215. Heretic (Bait book 3) (2021)
216. Anna's Sister (2021)
217. The Haunting of Quist House (The Rose Files 1) (2021)
218. The Haunting of Crowford Station (The Ghosts of Crowford 11) (2022)

AMY CROSS

219. The Curse of Rosie Stone (2022)
220. The First Order (The Chronicles of Sister June book 1) (2022)
221. The Second Veil (The Chronicles of Sister June book 2) (2022)
222. The Graves of Crowford Rise (The Ghosts of Crowford 12) (2022)
223. Dead Man: The Resurrection of Morton Kane (2022)
224. The Third Beast (The Chronicles of Sister June book 3) (2022)
225. The Legend of the Crossley Stag (The Ghosts of Crowford 13) (2022)
226. One Star (2022)
227. The Ghost in Room 119 (2022)
228. The Fourth Shadow (The Chronicles of Sister June book 4) (2022)
229. The Soldier Without a Past (Dead Souls book 14) (2022)
230. The Ghosts of Marsh House (2022)
231. Wax: The Complete Series (2022)
232. The Phantom of Crowford Theatre (The Ghosts of Crowford 14) (2022)
233. The Haunting of Hurst House (Mercy Willow book 1) (2022)
234. Blood Rains Down From the Sky (The Deal Trilogy book 3) (2022)
235. The Spirit on Sidle Street (Mercy Willow book 2) (2022)
236. The Ghost of Gower Grange (Mercy Willow book 3) (2022)
237. The Curse of Clute Cottage (Mercy Willow book 4) (2022)
238. The Haunting of Anna Jenkins (Mercy Willow book 5) (2023)
239. The Death of Mercy Willow (Mercy Willow book 6) (2023)
240. Angel (2023)
241. The Eyes of Maddy Park (2023)
242. If You Didn't Like Me Then, You Probably Won't Like Me Now (2023)
243. The Terror of Torfork Tower (Mercy Willow 7) (2023)
244. The Phantom of Payne Priory (Mercy Willow 8) (2023)
245. The Devil on Davis Drive (Mercy Willow 9) (2023)
246. The Haunting of the Ghost of Tom Bell (Mercy Willow 10) (2023)
247. The Other Ghost of Gower Grange (Mercy Willow 11) (2023)
248. The Haunting of Olive Atkins (Mercy Willow 12) (2023)
249. The End of Marcy Willow (Mercy Willow 13) (2023)
250. The Last Haunted House on Mars and Other Stories (2023)
251. 1689 (The Haunting of Hadlow House 1) (2023)
252. 1722 (The Haunting of Hadlow House 2) (2023)
253. 1775 (The Haunting of Hadlow House 3) (2023)
254. The Terror of Crowford Carnival (The Ghosts of Crowford 15) (2023)
255. 1800 (The Haunting of Hadlow House 4) (2023)
256. 1837 (The Haunting of Hadlow House 5) (2023)
257. 1885 (The Haunting of Hadlow House 6) (2023)
258. 1901 (The Haunting of Hadlow House 7) (2023)
259. 1918 (The Haunting of Hadlow House 8) (2023)
260. The Secret of Adam Grey (The Ghosts of Crowford 16) (2023)
261. 1926 (The Haunting of Hadlow House 9) (2023)
262. 1939 (The Haunting of Hadlow House 10) (2023)

263. The Fifth Tomb (The Chronicles of Sister June 5) (2023)
264. 1966 (The Haunting of Hadlow House 11) (2023)
265. 1999 (The Haunting of Hadlow House 12) (2023)
266. The Hauntings of Mia Rush (2023)
267. 2024 (The Haunting of Hadlow House 13) (2024)
268. The Sixth Window (The Chronicles of Sister June 6) (2024)
269. Little Miss Dead (The Horrors of Sobolton 1) (2024)
270. Swan Territory (The Horrors of Sobolton 2) (2024)
271. Dead Widow Road (The Horrors of Sobolton 3) (2024)
272. The Haunting of Stryke Brothers (The Ghosts of Crowford 17) (2024)
273. In a Lonely Grave (The Horrors of Sobolton 4) (2024)
274. Electrification (The Horrors of Sobolton 5) (2024)
275. Man on the Moon (The Horrors of Sobolton 6) (2024)
276. The Haunting of Styre House (The Smythe Trilogy 1) (2024)
277. The Curse of Bloodacre Farm (The Smythe Trilogy 2) (2024)
278. The Horror of Styre House (The Smythe Trilogy 3) (2024)
279. Cry of the Wolf (The Horrors of Sobolton 7) (2024)

AMY CROSS

For more information, visit:

www.amycross.com

AMY CROSS

Printed in Great Britain
by Amazon